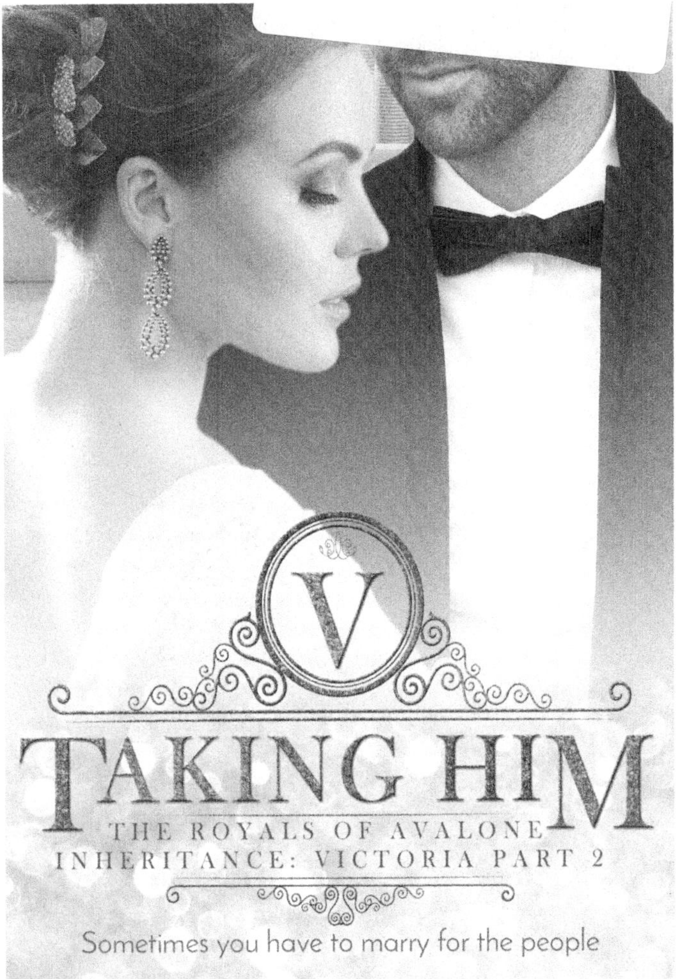
V
TAKING HIM
THE ROYALS OF AVALONE
INHERITANCE: VICTORIA PART 2
Sometimes you have to marry for the people
E.V. DARCY

TAKING HIM

THE ROYALS OF AVALONE - INHERITANCE: VICTORIA
PART 2

E V DARCY

Copyright © 2021 by E V Darcy

Cover Copyright © 2021 by Victoria Smith

All rights reserved.

This is a work of fiction. Names, characters, businesses, places, events and incidents are either the products of the author's imagination or used in a fictitious manner. Any resemblance to actual persons, living or dead, or actual events is purely coincidental.

All rights reserved. No part of this publication may be reproduced, distributed, or transmitted in any form or by any means, including photocopying, recording, or other electronic or mechanical methods, without the prior written permission of the publisher, except in the case of brief quotations embodied in critical reviews and certain other non-commercial uses permitted by copyright law. For permission requests, write to the publisher, addressed "Attention: Permissions Coordinator," at the address below.

info@evdarcy.com

For all those who dream of the perfect kiss

It takes hundreds of hours and thousands of dollars to produce a novel, so thank you for buying this book and supporting an author's dream.

If you got this book/ebook for free (outside of your local library) then this book has been pirated against the author's wishes.

Please enjoy immersing yourself into the world of Avalone and falling in love with the people of this unique nation.

King Richard VIII

Grand Duke Harold
- Prince Alistair of Avalone

Princess Helena
- Prince Spencer
- Prince Adam
- Princess Caroline

Duke Alfred
- Prince Leopold
- Prince John

Duke Frederick
- Prince Arthur
- Princess Rebecca
- Princess Francessca

Duke Augustus — Princess Grace
- Prince George
- Princess Grace

The first surviving Royal Twins

Princess Amelia
- Princess Jane
- Princess Elizabeth
- Princess Louise
- Prince Hugh
- Lady Alexandra

Princess Melinda
- Lady Philippa
- Lady Victoria
- Lady Henrietta

CHAPTER ONE

'mon, James!' Cormac shouted back into the flat as he jiggled the box he was holding to try and get a better grip. They didn't have much to take, but the few personal items they did have, he wanted to ensure they got to wherever they were going in one piece.

James was still pouting over the fact they had to move again, although Cormac failed to see exactly *why* his little brother was dawdling—anywhere had to be better than here. Cormac was not going to miss the tepid showers—even when he turned the temperature up to max. Or the hob he had to keep checking was off because he'd occasionally smell gas as he walked by. *Or* having to sleep on a sofa bed far too small for his large frame.

'I'm here,' James said with a tone Cormac had believed he wouldn't hear until his brother hit at least thirteen.

'Drop the attitude.' Cormac shifted the weight of the heavy box from one arm to the other. 'I don't know why you're moping so much about this. Think you'd be grateful to get a proper bedroom, more than likely with your own flat panel TV and all the consoles you'd ever want.'

James merely shrugged in response, pulling his little suitcase over the threshold, and heading towards the stairs. Cormac rolled his eyes and hoped his brother didn't trip over his own lip with how much it was sticking out.

'And that should just be those cases left then,' Cormac said to the two guys standing in the hallway. He'd told Victoria he didn't need a whole van, but she'd sent one anyway—even if it was on the smaller side. Their meagre possessions—a couple of suitcases, boxes of James' toys and books, his own smaller collection of fiction and textbooks, a box of a few personal bits, and the box in his arms filled with the only pictures and a couple of keepsakes he had left from his parents—looked rather sad and pathetic in the long-wheel-based Transit van.

'We'll follow you to the hotel,' one of the removal men told him. 'We'll take everything to your rooms there and then come back here for the rest. You said *everything* left here goes to a disposal site? Are you sure you don't want to donate some of it?'

Cormac shook his head. 'I got almost everything *from* charity stores years ago—if you're able to get them downstairs in one piece, I'll be amazed,' he confessed. The men grabbed the bags and hauled them up on their shoulders in a way that said they'd done this hundreds of times before. He let the two men go before him, so he could both lock up and not hold them up on the stairwell as he carefully made his way down with his box of treasures.

James sat on the kerb a few feet from the back of the van, his elbows resting on his knobbly knees and his hands cupping his face. He was kept company by his little suitcase carefully placed next to him. The picture was so pitiful it hurt.

Cormac sighed, shifting the box to hold it in one hand as

he reached down and ruffled James' hair, making a mental note it needed to be cut again.

'C'mon, buddy. Chin up. Whatever we're going to *is* going to be better than here. You do believe that, don't you?'

'Yeah,' James said glumly, making Cormac even more puzzled. But, with a very weary sigh for a six-year-old, James pushed himself to his feet and pulled his little case along the few feet to the back of the van where one of the removal men waited patiently for them. Reluctantly, Cormac handed the guy his box and watched as the man carefully put it into another, foam-lined, container. Cormac raised his brow.

'If we'd had time, sir, we'd have packed everything for you in these.' Cormac had to admit they did look a lot more secure than the cardboard ones he'd used.

'Is that to go in too, young sir?' the man crouched down and asked James, nodding towards his little suitcase.

'I suppose,' he said quietly with a little shrug.

Cormac moved to the front of the van, looking to see where Toby might be parked, but he couldn't see a Rolls Royce anywhere. Instead, he saw a sleek black car parked a few metres down on the opposite side of the road. Just as he spied the luxury sedan, it pulled out of its spot and made its way towards them.

As the Bentley Mulsanne pulled up, Cormac resisted the urge to open the door himself and climb inside, remembering how Victoria always waited for the driver. It seemed pointless when he had to wait and could easily just open the door himself, but if he was going to live in Victoria's world, he had to begin to follow her rules—even if he thought they were stupid.

'Whoa,' James said, taking in the shiny black car.

The younger Blake seemed more impressed with this one than the one they'd been in just two days ago. 'Can I sit in the front?'

'Afraid not,' Cormac said as the driver opened the rear door and ushered the pair inside.

It was a long journey for a six-year-old, even in a car as amazing as this one. After playing with every button James could reach, moving every knob and lever, switching through the TV channels on the small screen in front of him, the questions Cormac always dreaded started. And without knowing where they were going, he couldn't answer his brother's incessant *are we there yet?* And *how long now?*

'Dude, I *don't know*,' he said after the twelfth time. 'We'll be there when we get there.' Cormac saw the driver glancing his way in the rear-view mirror and Cormac knew he wasn't supposed to speak unless spoken to first. 'Hey, bud, sorry I didn't catch your name.'

'William, sir,' the driver said, his eyes quickly flickering to Cormac before refocusing on the road.

'Nice to meet you, Will. Could you tell us where we're going?'

'Sorry, sir, but I'm afraid that Lady Snape requested that I not reveal that information.' Cormac snorted. *Requested*. She'd probably demanded it. He still wasn't too sure which version of the woman he'd met was the real one, but he had to admit that he was kind of looking forward to finding out. Particularly if the real Victoria was the one he'd kissed in the back of the car.

The car twisted and turned its way through the capital's streets, hampered by the ever-present traffic cities seemed to be forever caught up in. But as the car turned down Main Street, Cormac's heart began to speed up, his breath caught in his throat. There was only *one* hotel on this street and there was no way they could be staying there. From his earlier days of taxiing through the capital, he knew the money that lined the pockets of the people who stayed there. It was where Heads of State were housed when they visited.

There was no way he could afford even the most basic of rooms at the Denyer Hotel.

But then *he* wasn't paying for it, and Victoria *was* a member of the Royal Family, where else would she stay if not in the country's finest hotel? He really needed to get his head around this whole thing and quickly.

The car slowed and pulled into the curved driveway of the most expensive and glamorous hotel in all Avalone. The Denyer hotel was known throughout the world as the height of luxury, and anyone who was anyone wanted to secure rooms—even a basic one—when they had the option, just to be able to say they were staying at such an establishment. His mouth fell open at the idea that he and James would be staying at such a place. Never in his wildest dreams would he have ever thought of stepping foot through the doors of the Denyer Hotel.

When he'd been a bellboy at a lower-end hotel—that he still couldn't afford to stay in—a few streets over, he and the bellboys from other hotels would hang around on lunch breaks, talking about who they'd seen that day, what type of tips they'd had, and so on, but the bellhops from the Denyer had never graced their breaks. They may have held the same job as them, but their bellboys—the cleaners too!—were all graduates, working their way up in the hotelier industry, desperate to be spotted by Niles Denyer one day.

'Look at those men in the weird hats.' James pressed his nose against the window to get a better look at the impeccably dressed doormen.

'I think you might have the wrong place,' Cormac said to the driver just before they stopped.

'No, sir.'

One of the doormen opened the car door and James almost tumbled out at the unexpected action. Without even glancing back at his older brother, he jumped from the car and stood on the pavement, head craned back to stare up at what seemed an impossibly tall building for a six-year-old.

'Whoa,' he breathed. 'Corrie, look.' He pointed up at the flags that billowed majestically with the breeze coming in from the ocean, high above the entrance.

'Yeah,' Cormac said distractedly, giving them a cursory glance as he peered around for the van with their belongings that had supposedly been following them.

'They've gone via the delivery entrance,' William told Cormac as he came around the car. 'They'll use the service lift to take your possessions up. Cormac's heart leapt into his mouth at the idea of his precious box being lost or dropped.

'Don't worry, sir, the men were personally chosen by Lady Victoria. Here'—the driver handed Cormac a small silver card—'show this to the lift attendant and they'll take you directly up.'

'I don't need to check in?' The other man shook his head.

'All taken care of, sir. I wish you well.'

Cormac lifted his hand in a half-hearted wave, his mind whirling with questions and self-doubts and the realisation he was *well* out of his depth.

'Corrie, is this where we're staying?'

'I guess so,' he said, his own head tilting back as he too became hypnotised by the dancing flags as he tried to get his brain around the fact.

'This is so... *cool!*' James exclaimed. 'Can we go in? Can we?'

His brother grabbed the hem of his t-shirt and tugged on it, fruitlessly trying to make Cormac move. Cormac looked down at the kid, noting his eyes were now bright with anticipation and wonder, eager to see what else awaited him. The grin that split wide across his face was a far cry from the pout that had graced his lips earlier, and he bounced on the balls of his feet, suddenly desperate to move and needing to do it quickly.

Cormac nodded and grabbed James' shoulder as he tried to race off into the grand building. He was fairly sure people who stayed here didn't run through throngs of people, darting around them as if they were an obstacle course.

'Hold my hand, bud.'

'Aww, Corrie—'

'No. No arguing on this. This isn't a place to run about in, and I don't want you getting lost.' He glanced down at the key card in his hand again; it seemed to shimmer in the morning sun. This was his way into something bigger and better for both James and himself, and if he was going to survive this for as long as he'd need to, he was going to have to throw himself into everything Victoria asked him to.

He squared his shoulders, fixed the neck on his t-shirt from where James had pulled it out of shape with his pleading, and stepped forward, telling himself he belonged here.

He flashed the doorman a smile and nodded to the older gentleman as the man held the large gold and glass door open for him.

'Good day, sir,' the man said. Cormac nodded his head at the guy.

He kept tight hold of James as they strode through the lobby. A few members of staff raised their eyebrows at him, dressed in a plain white t-shirt and faded jeans—that were clearly not designer—but he kept his head up high.

He'd almost reached the bank of lifts when a large gentleman, dressed in the colours of the hotel, stepped in their path, stopping them in their tracks. James stepped closer to his brother, and Cormac automatically pulled him against his side.

'Excuse me, sir.' The man's voice was deep, shaking the

very air around them, making Cormac's hair stand on end. 'Only guests are permitted to the rooms.'

Cormac cursed himself as he felt his brows raising high, and his cheeks heating up. People walking by and getting into the lifts he'd been heading towards were starting to pay attention to them, their eyes filled with judgement, finding him beneath them despite having no clue who he was or any connections he might have. Part of him wanted to tell them all he was about to marry into royalty, that they'd soon be lining up to catch a glimpse of him at the first royal wedding in over a quarter of a century, but he quickly stamped that part of himself down. The announcement wouldn't go out until Friday and if it got out before Victoria was ready for it, he'd ruin all her plans.

He quickly schooled his face into one of utter contempt, mirroring those around him. He kept his eyes on the man— probably security—as he brought the silver card up level with his face.

'I *am* a guest.'

The human barricade glanced towards the card before doing a double take. His olive skin paled and he quickly licked his lips, probably calculating the best way to get out of the mess he'd got himself into.

'I'm sorry, sir, I didn't realise. It's just... You're going to the wrong lift.' The man swallowed and pointed to another lift set across the lobby. It had a single width, silver door and surround, and was easily missed if you weren't specifically looking for it.

'Thank you. I haven't stayed here before and my assistant arranged the room.' The security-guy's own brows raised at that. 'She failed to pass on exactly where I was to go.'

'Of course, sir. Please let me know if there's anything you need. Anything at all.'

Cormac looked the man up and down, before nodding and turning to head to where he needed to go.

He glanced down at the card as he pressed the button, his head snapping up as the door slid open immediately. The operator inside jumped, scrambling to shove his phone deep in his pocket as he simultaneously tried to stand to attention. Cormac rolled his eyes before trying to step inside when the operator held out his hand to stop him.

'I'm sorry, sir. Platinum level only.'

Again, Cormac held up the card in his hand and the other man quickly nodded and stepped to one side to allow them access. Cormac glanced over to where the buttons usually were, surprised to see that there wasn't a list of floors as per usual. Instead, there were just two buttons, great big *platinum* —not silver—ones side by side.

'Your card please, sir,' the operator asked, holding out his hand. Cormac hesitated before handing it to him and watched with James, both curious as to what he needed it for, as he slid it into the slot under the two buttons. A ring of light highlighted one labelled as *up*.

'Next stop, Penthouse,' the operator said, pressing the lit-up button.

VICTORIA PUSHED THE FRAME A LITTLE TO THE LEFT BEFORE standing back to take it in. She shook her head, pushing it a little to the right. Her head tilted, her nose wrinkling with indecision as she considered its position. No, it still wasn't right. She nudged her finger behind the crystal frame and pulled it slightly out again on the left side. With a nod of her head, she was satisfied.

Ping! The lift trilled to say it was coming up and the nerves in Victoria's stomach burst into life. She hurried around the living room to be waiting at the lift when it reached the penthouse, before turning on her heel and walking in the opposite direction, ready to summon Merryweather to meet her guests.

No, not guests, she reminded herself. Cormac was her husband-to-be, her partner going forward. They were to be *equals*, and this and any other home they shared would be *theirs*, not hers.

She froze mid-step, uncertainty suddenly gripping her. If they were to be equals, then surely, she should be the one to greet them and welcome them home.

A second *ping* sounded to say they were halfway up, and Victoria cursed under her breath. She pirouetted one-hundred-and-eighty degrees and hurried back towards the entrance, pausing at the doorway to take a deep breath as the third and final ping sounded. Her whole body buzzed with the need to move, to do *something* as she waited for the door of the lift to slide open, but anyone watching her would never have noticed.

Hearing the door slide open—and James' exclamation of *cool!*—she stepped into the elevator vestibule with a smile.

'Good afternoon,' she said cheerfully, internally cringing at the false happiness in her voice. The two Blake brothers both turned to her, James with eager excitement in his eyes, clearly desperate to be free of his brother's vice-like grip on his shoulder so he could immediately run and explore, and Cormac who looked wholly unimpressed by the grandeur of the private lobby.

If a penthouse apartment with a private lift didn't impress him—or at least outwardly appear so—then perhaps he didn't need as much training as she thought. She made a note to mention such to her assistant, Kirstie, later.

'Hey, Victoria!' James practically shouted, waving to her

enthusiastically. 'Is this our place? I thought this was our place. Why are you here? Are you staying here too?'

'Dude, be chill,' Cormac said with a roll of his eyes. But Victoria merely chuckled at the boy's eagerness; it was nice to see someone who appreciated things. Too often, she was surrounded by people who were so used to such luxury that they took it for granted, for simply the norm. After visiting their much humbler abode this week, Victoria had been looking at her own surroundings and needs rather differently.

'It's okay, Cormac. You want a tour, James?'

'Do I!'

Victoria held out her hand to him, and James went to her willingly, sliding his own tiny palm into hers and gazing up at her with a bright, genuine smile. She couldn't help but return it, feeling it fill her and soothing the butterflies she'd been feeling all morning.

She made to lead him into the living area when James pulled back on her hand.

'You haven't said hello yet.' His little face frowned up at the two adults who stood a fair distance apart still.

'Hey,' Cormac said with a wave. She managed a smile to him. Okay, so he'd need *some* work.

'Hello.'

James' head swivelled between them, his frown deepening.

'You're supposed to kiss her, Corrie.' His young face pouted. 'Boyfriends and husbands *always* kiss their girl-friends or wives on their cheeks when they come home. And they say something like *Hi, honey, I'm home!*'

Cormac's brows raised as he stared down at his little brother and Victoria had to bite her lips between her teeth to stop herself from laughing.

'Where'd you hear that?'

'*Duh*,' James said with an eye-roll so dramatic, Victoria briefly wondered if he'd met Alexi already. 'It's in *all* the films, *and* on the telly.'

'Is it now?' Cormac's tone said he wasn't convinced by James' reasoning, but he approached Victoria anyway. Her smiled faltered, recalling vividly how she'd felt the last time he'd kissed her cheek in the back of the car, how she'd wanted him to pounce on her and show her what he really wanted to do. She practically salivated at the thought of being swept up in his arms, tasting him properly as he crushed her tightly against his chest and ran his hand down her back, under her bottom and grabbed her leg to bring up around his hip as she felt-

'Hi, honey, I'm home.' Cormac's lips pressed gently against her cheek and she felt his smile form as her breath hitched in her throat. 'Later, princess,' he murmured in her ear as he moved away. She caught his heated gaze as he stepped back, that lopsided smile of his curling up one corner of his mouth again, making promises she'd have to ensure he kept.

'Um,' James' little voice interrupted their moment together. He stared up at the two, clearly knowing something was happening, but not understanding exactly what it was. He looked adorable and Victoria couldn't help the little laugh that escaped her, making James frown even harder.

She gently pulled the young boy's hand, coaxing him to finally move. 'Come on, I got my *honey* and my kiss, now I'll show you around.' Her companion came willingly, his little legs hurrying to keep up with her naturally longer stride.

'So, this is the living room.' She held up her free hand to gesture around. It was an amazing room, decorated so tastefully that she was already making notes on when she finally got a chance to decorate her own place. Having lived in a royal residency most of her life, she'd never had a chance to put her own stamp on things. And she'd begun to realise she had no idea what she liked or wanted in a home.

'Whoa.' James dropped her hand and ran over to the floor-to-ceiling windows.

'Impressive, huh?' she said as Cormac came and stood beside her, his eyes fixed on the unimpeded view over the few buildings between them and the bay. She spied the *Queen Mary 2* carefully navigating the long strait that separated the beautiful golden beaches of the north side, twisting from the small city of Daven up towards the Continental highway, from the south side, home to tall sheer cliffs, that provided the deep waters ships needed to enter the pool and enabling them to dock in the capital city. The giant ocean liner's bow cut its way smoothly through the crystal clear, deep waters, heading to Avon's docks so its passengers could disembark for their day trips.

'Can't believe you rented the penthouse.' Cormac's voice was quiet, making Victoria glance over to him to ensure he was speaking to her and not just muttering to himself. His eyes cast her way as he waited for a response.

'The other suites were a little snug,' she began, keeping her own voice as quiet as his. 'I didn't think you'd want me on top of you guys as you adjusted.'

'Victoria, this is the biggest suite in all of Avon, hell, in the entire country. There are others out there that aren't as big and *still* would have given us room to spare. The Avoy, for example, has a presidential suite that's half this size, that would have suited fine.'

Although she was surprised by his knowledge of hotels, she considered his words, trying to pick out what he was really trying to say. Was it too extravagant for him? Did he think it a waste of money? He would obviously see money differently to the way she did after scrimping by all these years.

'The monthly rate is well within our housing budget,' she said with a hopeful lilt to her voice. Cormac opened his mouth to speak before closing it again, and she could see this time *he* was trying to fathom her meaning. She jumped in before he could say anything.

'Cormac, you don't need to worry about money anymore, let me take care of that.' She realised it was the wrong thing to say straight away as his confusion turned into outright annoyance.

'You don't have to *waste* money just because you have it,' he said. 'Somewhere less ostentatious would have been more than adequate.'

'I didn't mean—' She cut herself off as James glanced over at the two of them, his hazel eyes narrowing at the pair. She didn't want him to know that this was not the perfect little image he had from his TV shows and movies.

She chewed the right side of her lower lip as she considered the man next to her, who stood so close and was yet so far from her reach. How did she keep getting this so wrong? There had to be a way for Cormac to ease into her life and for her to somehow make him comfortable here... But that was the point; she was trying to make him *fit* into a lifestyle of *hers*. If she was going to be stepping out of the royal shadow, did she need to maintain the kind of life she had now? Could she find somewhere for them both to fit *together*?

He was right; just because she had such a large fortune, didn't mean she had to use it all... Maybe they could take up a smaller house than the ones she'd been looking at. Did they really need sixteen bedrooms? Ten would more than suffice, surely? She winced internally at the thought that Cormac might think they only needed three—one for each of them. But then, where would guests stay? How would their family grow?

'You're right,' she said quietly. 'This place is a little...

unnecessary. I just…' She sighed and took a seat on the beautiful purple and white sofa. 'This place is out of the way. It's secure. Only those with key cards can get up here and the only people with them are you and I, and the penthouse butler—'

'And the manager and security and—'

'No.' Victoria shook her head. 'None of them have access when there is someone in residence. Even the lift attendant can't get up here.'

Cormac rubbed his forehead as he took a seat on the opposite end of the couch. 'So, what if there's a fire?'

'That depends on where it is—on the north side, there's an escape room with a slide that goes down three stories to where the stairwells begin, and on the south side there's a stairwell that goes all the way to the middle of the building, where you again join the main escape plan. Both have no way into those sections at all. The doors are hidden and can only be opened on the inside.

'The lift up to this floor has only three access points other than the ground floor and the entrance way. The staff lift in the back is the same—different floors though—and that can only be called from up here.'

'Wait—so someone always lives here?'

'Yes, there has to be someone up here to call for the staff lift. When there's a resident here, there is always a butler present and only *he* can call up the staff lift. He's the only one with the key.'

'So, he lives with us until we check out?'

'Yes, he lives her permanently—it's why he's so well-paid.'

She watched as Cormac shook his head. 'Rich people,' he said with disgust. She took that as her opening.

'We should probably talk about our ideas for the future.' That got his attention as he looked towards her. 'Like the type of house we might be interested in…'

'Yeah, I guess.'

'Cormac!' James' startled voice caught both their attentions and Cormac was out of his seat and moving to him, before he realised his little brother was simply stood looking intently at the mantle above the fireplace.

Ah, he'd spied her surprise before she'd had the chance to reveal it herself.

She pushed herself to her feet and stepped towards the silent pair who were both openly staring at the pictures she'd set out just before their arrival.

Cormac moved forward and gently lifted the crystal frame she'd agonised over the placement of. It was the beautiful image of his parents on their wedding day, his mother a twenty-something beauty stepping down from the church steps on the arm of his father, laughing and smiling, not paying the camera the slightest bit of attention, too caught up in each other. It captured their love perfectly.

It made Victoria both smile and ache in longing and loss. She'd dreamt of a love that true and pure all her life, imagining looking at her own husband on her big day in a similar way. Now, she'd be lucky to get through the ceremony with a smile from him. But Cormac was already going above and beyond, giving up his freedom just for her. Asking for him to fall in love with her as well was clearly asking too much of her luck. And while she found him attractive—*really* attractive—who knew if she'd ever be able to fall in love with him either? They still had no idea who each other were, but at least they had time to find out.

She watched as he ran his finger over the delicate framework. She'd picked that one because it was simple yet elegant; it didn't detract from the beauty of the image, but it didn't do the photo a disservice either.

'How did you...?' Cormac asked, turning suddenly to her.

'I had William take a diversion,' she admitted. 'Made sure

he took the busier routes over the quicker ones the removal van took...' His brows raised at her confession.

'I'm so sorry,' she hastened to add. 'I just wanted there to be some part of home here waiting for you both. James' toys and books are already in his room, and your clothes and personal belongings are also away and... Well, the frames...' Most had been in hideously thin, cheap wooden frames that were more tape than wood. She'd had to get help to get the one of his parents out of the ratty frame because of the amount of tape on the corners and on the back, securing it in place. She hadn't wanted to damage the print.

Merryweather was a godsend.

'I recognised they were very precious to you. The removal men said that you wouldn't let them touch that particular box and were hesitant to even put it in the van. I completely understand your reluctance; they're all beautiful pieces.' She waved towards the rest of the room where some of his other treasured images were now sitting in their own beautiful frames, while the ones he couldn't see here, were proudly dotted throughout the rest of the suite, intermingled with her own.

'I didn't think the frames were going to hold up, so I had Merryweather send a staff member out for some new ones, that's when William may have taken a few roads he hadn't needed to...'

Cormac stared across the room at a few other pictures before glancing back down at the one in his hand. Victoria played with her necklace, pulling and sliding the pendant along the delicate chain as she waited for him to speak, to say something either way.

'Thank you,' he whispered, and she noted the small catch in his throat. 'It had originally been in a pretty frame—solid silver. I- I had to pawn it...'

'If you'd prefer it in silver...' She turned to reach for the intercom to call the butler when Cormac quickly said *no*.

She turned back to him to see a bright smile on his lips, his eyes shimmering a little, and Victoria had to swallow down the sudden lump in her own throat.

'This...' He held the picture to his chest. 'This is perfect. Thank you.'

'You're welcome, Cormac.'

And in that moment, Victoria had hope that the dreams she'd carried as a child, may still come true...

IT WAS LATE AND JAMES WAS STARTING TO DRIFT OFF AT THE table after such a long and exciting day. They'd had lunch on the terrace not long after their arrival and he and James had discovered the penthouse came with its own pool that ran the width of the building, splitting into two wider infinity pools at either end. And despite his previous misgivings, Cormac couldn't help but wonder if it was possible to add a pool to their wish list when looking for their home; just because he didn't think they should blow *all* their money didn't mean he couldn't have a few wild luxuries.

James loved to swim, and he began bouncing as soon as he saw the pool running along next to their perfectly set up table. He'd had to promise his brother they'd take a dip *after* they'd eaten, and thus after lunch—and once their stomachs had settled—their swimwear had miraculously appeared in the little changing huts on the other side of the pool. The next three hours had been spent chasing James around the pool and entertaining him... *After* Cormac had got over his initial reaction to Victoria in her bikini.

He'd walked out of the changing hut and seen her lying on a lounger already, her peachy skin radiant in the hot afternoon sun. Her breasts were barely concealed in tiny scraps of fabric that constituted the top and the bottom part... Well, there was *no* bottom when she'd turned over to catch the sun on her back. He'd had to swim for a few minutes to calm his raging hard-on after noticing the perfect globes of her arse on display for all to see. He was going to have to speak to her regarding such outfits. Around adults, not an issue—hell, he'd seen far more when stripping!—but around James, a six-year-old, she needed to wear a little more.

Then after some more food and seeing the giant TV the living room offered, James had plonked himself there, and they'd ordered several child-appropriate films. Now he had a sleepy little brother tucked in his arms, head lolling against his shoulder as they climbed the stairs to the second floor of the suite.

The top of the stairs opened into another large sitting area with bookcases filled from floor to ceiling with all sorts of books. He itched to look at the titles on the volumes and see if they had anything interesting. He'd love to be able to lose a few hours in a good book now he was unemployed...

Crap, that was another thing he had to figure out. What was he going to do with his time?

'This is the snug,' Victoria said to him quietly. 'I suppose it could also be counted as a library.' But she didn't sound too impressed by that thought. Cormac imagined she had a library as big as the one in Disney's *Beauty and the Beast* back in her castle or wherever it was she lived. He supposed not much could impress you if you lived in a castle, a palace or... what had she said? A hall? He'd have to look up what exactly a *hall* was.

His list of things to learn was growing quickly.

'And this is James' room.'

'Where are you going to sleep?' the young boy asked

groggily as he lifted his head to look at the door to his new bedroom.

'Cormac is in the room next door to you.' She pointed down the hallway to a door that faced them. 'There's a bathroom that joins your rooms together. If you need him in the night, you just have to walk through the bathroom and open his door.'

That comment made James pull back from Cormac to stare at Victoria as she stood poised to open his bedroom door in a *ta-da!* moment.

'And you? You'll sleep there too?'

'Um, my room is just over there.' She motioned to a door on the opposite side of the hallway that was about midway between the two brothers. Cormac watched James' face take on that befuddled look he got when something inside his brain couldn't connect the dots to something he knew he should understand. It was basically when his big brain was about to drop Cormac in it with someone.

'But you're getting married,' the boy said, all traces of sleepiness gone. 'And husbands and wives share a room. Right, Corrie?' He turned to Cormac, his frown so pronounced that Cormac swore the kid was going to have wrinkles before he hit puberty.

'Err, well—'

James' hazel eyes narrowed as they darted between the two of them.

'Of course,' Cormac finished and Victoria did a double take at him. 'It's just Victoria thought you'd want me to sleep next to you for a while just in case—'

'I'm fine!' James' eyes quickly went wide, and he shook his head. Subtlety was not the kid's strongest point and Cormac knew he didn't want his little bedtime problem revealed to Victoria. 'I don't need you sleeping next to me.' He pushed at

Cormac's shoulders, meaning he wanted to be put down. Cormac rolled his eyes as he complied.

'C'mon then, let's see this fancy pad you got,' Cormac declared, and Victoria quickly turned the handle, letting the door swing open. The room was lit by soft lamplight, to show a crisp white room with deep blue accents. But it was the size of the room that made Cormac stare, his mouth hanging open like a cartoon character.

It was *huge*. Probably twice the size of the whole flat they'd left behind. It had a bed far too big for tiny James, the same floor-to-ceiling windows as downstairs, but these were draped with beautiful curtains, while an enormous cupboard —that he knew had a fancy name—was positioned opposite the bed. There were some comfortable-looking chairs and a big, beautiful desk sat facing the window.

Cormac frowned, unable to see where a wardrobe was.

Where had they put James' clothes?

'So, you have your own television,' Victoria said, heaving open the doors on the cupboard.

'Whoa!' James breathed the word as he saw the massive TV set.

'And I think it comes with... Ah yes!' Victoria pulled down one of the fronts of what Cormac had thought was a drawer. Instead, it was a little compartment... for a game console.

Cormac sighed, but it was lost over James' squeal of delight. All traces of sleep wiped from him. Cormac shook his head; they were never going to get him out of the room now.

'You should have access to any game you want, as long as it's available on this model, the hotel said. If it's not...' She opened another identical fake drawer next to the first to show the console's main rival machine. This time, Cormac's groan was audible, but the other two ignored him. 'It should be on this one, right?'

'Yes!' James reached up and took the proffered console controller from Victoria's hands. 'Thank you!'

'Well, you can play whenever you want—as long as it's okay with your brother.'

'*After* schoolwork,' Cormac told James, as he took the controller from the boy's little fingers and put it back on the shelf. 'And not right before bed.'

'But, Corrie!' James tried, but Cormac shook his head.

'PJ's and bed for you, mister.' When Victoria saw him looking around the room for a clue to where his clothes would be, she jumped in to help.

'Your clothes are through this door.' Victoria opened one of the two doors on the otherwise empty wall. Cormac and James poked their heads inside and saw a dressing room that probably was the same size as their old flat.

'And this is your bathroom.' She pushed the other door open and showed off the sparkling white en-suite the room had. A toilet, separate bath, shower and... *two* sinks? He figured he was supposed to use this room as well, but why did they need a sink *each*?

'Go use the loo,' Cormac said, nudging James into the bathroom. 'I'll grab your pyjamas and we'll get you all tucked in.' James sighed, as if suffering a hardship as he marched into the bathroom and closed the door behind him. Cormac put his foot in its way so it didn't click close—he didn't want the kid to accidentally lock himself inside—before he disappeared into the fancy dressing room.

'Um, are you really staying with me?' Victoria asked as he began to rummage through the drawers, trying to find a set of Spider-Man pyjamas he knew James liked.

'Yeah, I'll have to,' he said without thinking. 'If James comes looking for me in the night because he's had an accident—' He glanced up at her. 'Ah, yes, he, um, he occasionally wets the bed. Merryweather should probably know about that, so he can be prepared for the extra washing.'

'I'll see to it.' She chewed on her lower lip as he continued to look for the set he wanted. When he couldn't, he grabbed a Hulk set he knew would be just as acceptable. He'd have to have a good look through this place in the morning to see where everything was.

'Anyway, yeah, if he comes looking, he'll go to your room now you've pointed it out, and if I'm not there...' He sighed, his shoulders slumping as he stared up at the ceiling for strength. 'There will be no end to the questions, trust me.'

'Okay, well, I guess I should arrange to have your clothes moved then,' she said, turning on her heel and walking out of the room.

Cormac stared after her, wondering what he'd done to—

Oh, crap. The realisation hit him. He'd just invited himself to sleep with her. He was a freaking idiot. He went to chase after her, to say that he would happily sleep on the floor—maybe they could bring in a cot-bed?—when James appeared around the door, looking very tired again.

'Corrie, can I go to bed now?' he asked, rubbing his eyes.

'Sure, kiddo, let's get you changed.'

CORMAC PAUSED AT THE DOORWAY TO VICTORIA'S BEDROOM, hand on the handle. He pressed his forehead against the cool wood of the door and tried to wrestle his mind into some sort of submission. He'd had a whirlwind of a day with the move and running around after James to keep him entertained and stop him from asking too many questions. Add that to the reason *why* they'd moved in in the first place; he'd barely slept after O'Malley had shown up, too frightened the dick would return.

Right now, he just wanted to crash in a bed—God, he really wanted a *bed* and not a floor after all—and sleep for the next twenty hours or so, just to rest and recharge. But first, he had to go in and apologise to Victoria for invading her space.

Although, with the way she'd looked at him earlier, he didn't think she'd be too averse. And if he wasn't so tired, he'd have certainly obliged his princess, but he just... was. He huffed at himself. How many twenty-five-year-olds turned down a hot, sexy woman who was waiting in bed for them?

Cormac took a deep breath before straightening up and squaring his shoulders, and with another breath, he opened the door.

'Oh, there you are,' Victoria said, glancing up from a chair where she was curled up with a book and a soft-looking blanket. Cormac blinked, taking in the scene before him. He'd been expecting her in some sort of negligée, maybe a pair of those stockings he'd caught a glimpse of the other day, but instead, she was dressed in a pair of flannel pyjamas that hung a little long on her arms, covering her fingers.

'I, er...' He glanced around the room, noting that it was a *sitting* room rather than a bedroom. 'I thought this was your bedroom?'

'It's the master suite,' Victoria explained. 'I didn't think you two would want me in your space all the time, so I took this one.' She bit her lip and glanced down in embarrassment. 'I hope you don't mind.'

There was a suite *within* a suite? Cormac shook his head in disbelief, but Victoria took it as an answer to her question.

'Oh, good, but I suppose it worked out well if we're actually to share.'

'About that,' he began, but was stopped by a knock at the

door. Victoria stood up, carefully put her book down and padded over to answer. Cormac noted the length of her pyjama bottoms were like the sleeves of her top, just slightly too long; the back of them slipped under her heel as she walked, and the front almost hid her toes.

He couldn't see who it was at the door, but Victoria spoke quietly to them, so he took the chance to have a better look around. The window behind Victoria's chair of choice was a set of French doors that led to a private terrace overlooking the city towards the glistening waters of the bay. The moon was high and bright in the sky, illuminating the deeper and darker waters as it reached out towards the Atlantic, and Cormac really understood why people paid so much for such a view. Who wouldn't want to see this day in and day out?

He pulled his head back inside and made his way across the room to where a set of double doors stood closed. He carefully eased them open and almost groaned with happiness at the sight of a bedroom, complete with what he assumed was the biggest bed in the whole world. Two lights on either side of the bed bathed the room in a soft, warm glow, and only beckoned him towards the fluffy, feather-lined all the more.

'Tired?' Victoria's quiet voice asked, making him jump. He turned to see her standing at a small table, placing a silver tray with two overly full mugs of something hot. 'I figured you must be exhausted,' she continued as she picked up one of the drinks. 'I asked Merryweather for something to help us sleep.'

She passed a mug of thick, frothy, dark chocolatey drink to him before turning and taking her own.

'My mum was an ambassador for tea. Thought that anything and everything could be solved with a good cup, brewed to perfection.' She came back over to him as she spoke and opened the doors he'd just been peeking through.

She flicked a switch at one side and the soft lights in the sitting room went out, leaving them to the enticing allure of the bed lamps.

'*But*,' she continued as she padded her way into the bedroom and put her cup down on the right-hand nightstand. 'For sleeplessness, if you were tired and in need of a good night's sleep, tea was *not* the solution. A perfect hot chocolate, mixed with cocoa, and made with the creamiest of milks was the only answer then.' She nodded to him, and he raised the mug to his lips.

He heard the deep, almost pornographic groan of pleasure before he realised it was him making it as the magical concoction hit his tongue. A perfect blend of sweet milky chocolate with a hint of smooth darkness filled his mouth and exploded over his taste-buds in a way nothing ever had before.

'I'm the only one—' She cut herself off as she considered something, her nose wrinkling. 'Well, and now Merryweather, who know the exact recipe for this. Luckily, he has so many NDA's slapped into his contract, I know he'll never make it for anyone again, unless one of us asks him to.'

'It's amazing,' he said. He took another long pull of the milky drink. Victoria smiled, a wide bright smile, before she walked around the enormous bed and began playing with the covers.

'I couldn't find any sleepwear for you,' she told him.

'I usually just sleep in my boxers,' he confessed, stepping forward as the bed whispered to him. 'But I can put some sweatpants on if you want?'

'Cormac, we're going to be *married*. If you want to sleep naked, you can.'

'Do you sleep naked?' he asked, hearing the slurring of his words and he began to struggle to keep his eyes open. He sat heavily on the end of the bed and took another gulp of his drink.

'Sometimes,' she answered honestly. 'But I don't think tonight's that kind of night.' She came before him and gently took the mug from his hand.

'Is there something in that?' he asked, his eyes focused on the cup as she put it on the cabinet of what he assumed would be *his* side of the bed. 'Something to *make* me fall asleep? I wouldn't try anything like that. I'm not that sort of guy,' he said quietly, casting his eyes down to the floor. Her feet came into view again as she stood back in front of him and gently lifted his chin with her finger.

She smiled softly at him as his green eyes met her caramel gaze.

'I know you wouldn't, Cormac. Of anyone in the world, I feel safest with you. And, no, there's nothing in the cup other than what I said, chocolate, cocoa, and milk. You're just that tired and the warmth of the milk is lulling you further.' She dropped to her knees in front of him and he couldn't help the smile that automatically curled his lips.

'On our first date, Princess?' he said and chuckled at exasperated shake of her head.

'Technically, this would be our third,' she told him as she reached down and removed his socks from his feet. She threw them across the floor before she smirked back up at him and went for his belt. She began to unbuckle it, and Cormac took in a sharp breath as her hands grazed his crotch. If she wasn't careful, she wasn't just going to wake him up again, but his little soldier too.

'But no,' she said as she finally got his belt free and unbuttoned his jeans. 'I just want to get you comfortable and get you into bed.'

'You doing *that* isn't going to make me comfortable…'

'Okay,' she said, sitting back on her heels, her hands

running down his thighs to his knees before they fell away. 'Then you do it and let's get you into bed.'

He stared down at her, their eyes meeting as he considered his wife-to-be.

Her parted lips and the slight flush to her cheeks told him that if he were to ask for more, she'd be willing to give it. And although his heart was willing, and his libido most certainly interested, his body was just too damn tired. He smiled down at her, reaching out and brushing a stray lock of hair behind her ear.

'Okay, Princess. But no ravishing me in the night, okay?' He winked as he slowly climbed back up to his feet and shimmied his trousers down his legs. She stared up at him, keeping her eyes on his the whole time, and Cormac had never found something so sexy before. She didn't move to touch him, didn't even glance at his suddenly interested cock, but he *felt* her.

He pulled his t-shirt over his head and dropped it to the floor beside her and still she kept her eyes on his. He knew she was dying to look, to take in his body, to run her hands over him... He wondered if she was as turned on as he was—even if he wasn't able to physically show it right now. He'd never hated being so exhausted as he was at that moment.

'Are you going to tuck me in?' he whispered as he offered his hand to help her to her feet. She rose so gracefully, in one smooth motion, and stood so close to him.

'Do I get a goodnight kiss?' she asked, her own voice hushed.

How can I refuse? How could I refuse her anything? he wondered as he traced his fingers along her cheek before gently cupping the back of her head. She willingly submitted to him, turning her head ever so slightly as he lowered his mouth to hers.

It was as soft as the kiss she'd pressed to him days ago,

and she mewed in displeasure when he pulled back ever so slightly to take her in. Her dark lashes caressed her cheek as she fluttered her eyes open, her lip pouting when she knew he wasn't going to kiss her the way she wanted.

'When I kiss you properly, Victoria, it won't end there.'

She took in a deep shaking breath before asking, 'Promise?'

'Oh, I promise,' he said, pressing his lips to her nose. 'So, you better make sure we're alone and neither of us is tired.'

Smiling up at him, she took his hand in hers and stepped back before leading him to his side of the bed and gently pushing him down onto the luxurious bed. He snuggled deep into the mattress, moaning in pleasure; after years on a too-small-for-him sofa bed, this was heaven. He caught the delighted warmth in her eyes, as she pulled the thick, fluffy duvet over him and pressed a kiss to his forehead.

'Sweet dreams, my handsome prince,' Victoria whispered, and before she'd even moved away, his eyes closed and he was asleep.

CHAPTER TWO

Victoria woke as a single ray of light made its way through the gap between the thick blackout curtains that otherwise shrouded the room in darkness.

She was cocooned in warmth, a combination of the luxury covers—far better than those at Renfrew Hall—and the fact that Cormac had his arm wrapped tightly around her waist, pulling her into the curve of his body.

She smiled sleepily into the pillow, burying her head into it even more, as she tried to settle back into a happy, contented sleep. Last night had been lovely. She'd been amazed at how quickly he'd fallen asleep and how peaceful he'd looked. The stress that lined his eyes was smoothed away and the permanent hint of a frown disappeared completely, making him look younger than his twenty-five years. It had momentarily worried her that she was marrying someone so much younger, but Cormac had survived every hardship life had thrown at him and overcome every adversity he'd needed to, that his maturity was far greater than his age.

Cormac mumbled something in his sleep and pressed his

lips against her neck, making her grin wider... Until he squeezed her closer. The sharp press on her bladder reminded her that *she* wasn't as young as she used to be!

She carefully untangled herself from his arms, still grinning as he made a little grumble at the loss of his life-size snuggle pillow, and tiptoed her way to the en-suite bathroom. When she came back in, Cormac's head was partly under the pillow and he'd twisted himself up good and proper in the duvet. Deciding not to disturb him, and to answer her rumbling stomach, she stepped into the dressing room and got herself ready for the day before going to check on her little brother-in-law.

She knocked quietly on the door and waited for James' muffled permission to enter.

'Good morning, James,' she said as she peeked her head inside and saw that the six-year-old was already up, dressed, and engaged in a game on one of the consoles. She glanced towards his dressing room as she stepped inside and saw, through the ajar door, clothes strewn about. Merryweather's staff were going to complain. She'd have to speak to the butler later and apologise for causing him problems—it might be their jobs, but it was always best to keep the staff on side.

'I'm late for school,' he told her without looking up. Her frown deepened, and she worried her lip. She'd forgotten about that, and apparently, so had Cormac.

'You get a day off for moving to a new house,' she fibbed. 'It's to let you settle in.'

'Awesome!' was his reply. Victoria wasn't sure if he was saying that about being able to miss school or blowing the head off a zombie on screen.

'Do you want to come down for breakfast?'

'What're we having?' he asked, throwing a glance her way before he refocused back on his game. She frowned at that.

Cormac had let him get into bad habits in that regard, and she made a note to ask Kirstie to arrange some basic lessons for James as well.

'Well, what would you like? We have a chef here who can cook a range of things; why don't we go look?'

'Where's Corrie?' he asked, pressing his button as he held the controller closer to the TV. Victoria wondered if that made it work better.

'Still sleeping,' she answered. She watched the TV set as his character fired a gun at some sort of creature that was trying to get him. As the thing exploded in a shower of blood and guts that spattered the TV from the inside, Victoria decided enough was enough. These games were *not* for six-year-olds.

She'd have the hotel put an age block on the consoles.

'That's enough of that.' She reached out and took the controller from his small hands.

'Hey!' he protested and tried to snatch it back, but she was too quick. 'I was playing that!' He scrambled off the bed and tried to make it to the armoire, but Victoria already had the controller in the fake drawer and was locking it with the key before he reached her. He scowled up at her and suddenly she was sixteen all over again, and having to deal with a pouting Alexi.

'Not anymore.' She said the words firmly, but not unkindly. 'Cormac said *after* schoolwork, and while you might be finishing school for summer next week, there are plenty more lessons for you to learn.'

'Like what?' His voice filled with open hostility.

'Well, about my family for a start. You do know who my family is, right?'

'Yeah, King Richard and Queen Katrine are your grandparents.'

'That's right, and my aunts and uncles are dukes and

princesses and there are rules that go with meeting them and talking to them, and so many other things.'

James' frown turned less scowl and more into one of consideration.

'Why?' he asked.

'Let's talk about it over breakfast. I'm *dying* for a cup of tea.' She made it sound so melodramatic, but she really needed to distract the boy from his video games.

'I don't like tea,' he told her, turning his nose up at her comment.

'If you've only ever tasted your brother's brews, I completely understand why you don't.' He snorted at that, his shoulders jumping as he huffed. 'Tea should *not* be made from a bag.'

'Then what do you use?'

'Tea should be brewed from leaves, in a teapot, never just in a cup—' She paused as she recalled Cormac handing her the overly large mug. 'And *definitely never* a mug.'

His little face lit up, his mouth making an *oh* shape before he said, 'Brewed? Like Professor Snape brews the potions in Harry Potter? Isn't *your* name Snape?'

'Um, yes.' She didn't want to confess she'd never read the popular books nor seen the films, although she remembered Marcus talking of them—he'd been a big fan.

'Can you show *me* how to brew tea?'

'Um.' She was completely lost of words. She certainly hadn't expected eager anticipation from him over a cup of tea, but a small curl of warmth filled her soul. Her own mother had taught her about tea at James' age and while James might not be her child, she was going to be the best thing he had to a mother figure.

'Sure, why not!' she said, holding out her hand to him. He beamed brightly at the outstretched limb and grabbed at it as he followed along beside her.

'And afterwards, could we go swimming again?'

'Okay,' Victoria agreed, in a bit of a daze at how quickly the boy ran from hot to cold and back again, as James began to tell her all about his swimming lessons at school.

∼

'Okay, so tell me everything we need.' Victoria asked as she gave her napkin a little flick to open it and rested it gently over her lap. 'Point to it as you say it so I can see you know which items you're talking about and not just reeling off names.'

James took a deep breath before he took his hands out of his lap where they'd sat fisted up while he watched Merryweather lay out the table.

'Teapot, canister to store the tea leaves, sugar bowl, milk pot-'

Milk pot?

James' head snapped to look up at her as she looked down at him with a raised questioning brow. His surprised face turned into one of consternation as he tried to recall what names she'd given to everything as it had been put out.

'Cream jug.' He nodded his head firmly as he touched it with the tip of his finger.

'Excellent. Okay, continue.'

'Tea strainer and its caddy, cup and saucer, and teaspoon.' He held the silver caddy spoon aloft as it were a trophy. The morning sun that bathed the terrace where they sat, caught it, and made it sparkle. She didn't have the heart to correct him just yet on that one.

'Fantastic!' she gave him a smile and an encouraging nod of the head. 'Okay, so now I'm going to show you how to brew the tea. First,' she said, reaching for the already warmed teapot and bringing it to them so he'd be able to see everything she was doing from where he knelt on the chair. They'd have to look at getting some sort of booster seat for him for going forward.

'You have to make sure you have a warm teapot—Merryweather already warmed this for us—and you need water.' The butler appeared at her side with a kettle wrapped in a towel. 'It should be fresh off the boil. Merryweather is going to add this for us, so we don't burn ourselves.'

James leaned away from the action, sliding his arms along the table as he went. Victoria was glad the staff hadn't added a tablecloth.

'Okay,' she said as the butler stepped back and left them to their lesson. 'Now we add the tea leaves.' James gripped the caddy spoon harder as Victoria opened the tea canister and held it out to him. 'We need one spoonful for each of us.' He carefully scooped out two spoons and dropped them into the steaming water. 'And an extra one for the pot.'

He glanced up at her, making sure he heard her right, before scooping out another. He made this one larger than the last and Victoria was curious about his thinking but kept her questions to herself so she didn't put him off. It would be a little stronger than she'd thought they would make for his first time, but he'd soon learn to adjust to taste this way.

'Now'—she put the lid on the pot—'we leave it for a few minutes.'

'How many?' James asked looking up at her, his neck right back as she put the pot further onto the table so he couldn't accidentally touch it.

'About five, but if you want a weaker tea, you could leave it for three or four.' He frowned at that and Victoria had a feeling he liked very precise answers. 'Tea is something that will become very personal to you,' she said as she nodded to Merryweather to begin serving breakfast. The two footmen stepped forward and removed the large silver cloches from the platters on the adjoining table that would serve as their buffet spread.

James practically vibrated in his chair as he saw the dishes of sausages, bacon, and eggs on one side of the table, while pancakes, waffles and pastries decorated the other. A vast array of syrups and fruit made a centrepiece in between the options. Victoria had a feeling their tea brewing would quickly be forgotten by her young apprentice.

James' eyes lit up as Merryweather began to help him make his plate, asking the young master what he wanted to eat. Victoria didn't believe for one second that Cormac had ever let his brother go hungry, although he'd probably allowed himself to miss a few meals more than he should have in order for James to have a full stomach. She wondered if his tiny frame was from a lack of good food over anything else. Cormac was far taller than the average Avalonian man who generally stood just below six foot, and he was broad so surely James should be similar in nature?

She pondered the thought as she made a few selections from the buffet herself, making sure there was a good helping of everything.

'Could you take this to Mr Blake, please?' she asked one of the waiting footmen. She intended for Cormac to enjoy a good breakfast in bed, but her good intentions were laid to waste when a sleepy Cormac stepped out onto the patio dressed in jeans and a t-shirt, yawning and scratching his head through his fluffed-up hair.

'Good morning,' she said as she waved away the footman and set the plate in the third place. She rose as Cormac joined them at the table and she pressed a kiss to his cheek.

'Mornin'' he replied with a bashful grin as he scooted the chair closer. His eyes surreptitiously glanced towards the waiting staff, and Victoria felt his immediate discomfort.

He'd have to overcome that soon, but she'd make an allowance for now.

'That will be all, thank you,' she said to Merryweather, who merely dipped his head in a bow. The other staff quickly disappeared and the butler finished tending to his young charge before also leaving them be.

'Are there always so many people about? Man, this looks good!' He didn't give Victoria a chance to answer before he grabbed his knife and fork and began hacking into his food. 'I'm starving!'

'Are you going to inhale it or eat it?' she asked, staring at him in horror as he shoved his overloaded fork into his mouth and swallowed almost immediately. The second forkful he had halfway to his mouth in anticipation, paused as he turned to her and then to his brother who stared at him with his mouth agape.

'Guess now wouldn't be a bad time for one of those lessons?' he said quietly as he slowly lowered his fork.

Victoria shook her head. 'Lesson one, actually *chew* your food. That way, you won't die before your time. Otherwise, this is a buffet breakfast. Quite simple, very casual,' she said as she reached for the teapot. 'You serve yourself, and you have very few utensils, but there are staff nearby should you need them.'

Cormac nodded along with each thing she said.

'Tea?'

'Wait!' James shouted, before tucking his chin to his chest. 'Sorry, I mean,' he said with a much more respectable tone of voice. 'I thought *I* was brewing.'

Victoria beamed at him. 'Of course.' She put the pot back down on the corner of the table between them. 'What we need is your cup and the tea strainer.'

James grabbed his little cup with both hands, clearly

frightened of dropping it, and put it carefully down in front of the pot, then took the strainer from its caddy.

'Looks like a mini-sieve,' he commented as he held it up towards one of his eyes and peered through it.

'Because it is,' Victoria told him as she plucked it from his fingers before it landed on the floor. She placed it across his cup. 'It goes across like this and it's going to stop you from having any leaves floating in your cup if they happen to drop through the spout. Now I'll pour,' she told him as she lifted the hot pot again. 'Watch how I do it.'

She moved the pot in small circles first, allowing the tea within to swirl, then she slowly began to pour the tea into the cup before she raised it a little higher and tipped it so the brew flowed faster, before dropping it down again.

'Does that help?' he asked, moving his hand up and down as she had done with the teapot.

'I don't know,' she shrugged, and then grinned at him. 'But it's fun.'

James smiled back at her over the top of his tea. 'Can I add the milk?' His voice was just a whisper, as if he was sharing the secrets of a special potion.

'This is a very special secret,' she said, dropping her own voice to match his. 'But milk can either make tea or ruin it. Strong teas do well with milk, but lighter teas or green teas don't.'

'Don't you add the milk first?' Cormac's voice interrupted their little lesson, and Victoria stared at him aghast at the suggestion.

'I beg your pardon?' she asked, sitting up straight in her chair, praying she hadn't just heard what she thought she had.

'Milk, it goes in first.' He repeated as he bit into a piece of toast.

Victoria closed her eyes and counted to three before opening them again.

'What?' Cormac huffed through his mouthful of toast. 'It makes the tea creamier.'

'You, Cormac Dean Blake, are a heathen. Milk goes in *after* the tea is poured.'

'Yeah, Corrie,' James jumped in to defend her. Cormac's eyes shifted between the two of them before shaking his head with a smile.

'Whatever. You're both nuts.'

'I've never been so insulted, James,' she said, turning back to her protégé. 'I don't know how you've put up with him.'

'Me neither,' James agreed solemnly, shaking his own head slowly as he looked at his brother with something akin to pity. Victoria had to bite her lip to stop from laughing, but it was only short-lived as a toast crust flew across her vision and bonked James right on the forehead.

'Hey!' James protested as Victoria's head whipped around to stare at Cormac in horror.

'Oh, lighten up, you two,' Cormac said, returning to his food.

Victoria helped James to add his milk and watched him take a sip. His eyes grew wide with surprise and pleasure, and he made an *mmm* sound before carefully putting the cup back on its saucer and tucking into his breakfast plate. Merryweather had piled it high with a bit of everything on offer, and the young boy was eager to sample the lot by the looks of things.

The trio settled into breakfast well, Victoria advising of their itinerary for the day; she had some appointments to attend, to firmly fix plans for the wedding, while Cormac and James were going off to buy clothes.

'They'll expect you there at two o'clock,' she advised Cormac. 'Oh, and this is for you.' She pulled the bag from under the chair that had arrived as she'd settled James down for breakfast.

Cormac peeked into the bag in curiosity before groaning.

'What's wrong? I assure you it's the best one out there.'

'I figured,' Cormac said as he pulled the box out of the bag that showed a sleek smartphone, made exclusively for the Royal Family with all the latest security protocols. 'I just— Why do I need this?'

'Because we have a lot to do, so we need to keep in touch. Also, I'll be putting *your* number down for things to do with James—like *school* applications,' she whispered the last part. She wasn't sure that James was aware he wouldn't be returning to his old school after next week. 'Also, for days like today—when he *misses* school and you need to *call* them to explain.'

The way Cormac's face turned bright red, the tips of his ears turning an endearing shade of pink, she knew she was right; he hadn't even thought about James being absent from school this morning. She made a note to get James' attendance records and see if that was a regular thing or not.

'Look I underst—'

A quiet cough from the living room doors caught her attention.

'Yes, Merryweather?'

'My lady, Mr Carter, the hotel manager, has called to say your sisters are downstairs and are making a fuss at the front desk. He wants to know if you'd like them to be sent up or if you'd like him to *deal* with the situation?'

Victoria frowned. Why were her sisters here? *How* did her sisters know where she was?

She dabbed her mouth with her napkin before putting it over her plate and standing up.

'Please have them sent up.' The butler nodded before turning and doing as she bid.

'Why are you sisters here?' Cormac asked, pushing his own plate away.

'I don't know,' she confessed as she grabbed the back of the chair for support. 'But I have a sinking feeling something has gone wrong.'

∽

AND, BOY, HAD SOMETHING GONE WRONG.

Victoria anxiously glanced towards Cormac as she heard her sisters spilling out of the lift, while waiting for them in the living room. They'd banished James off to his room, but Victoria kept glancing towards the stairs just in case—at least she hadn't yet put the game blocks on the consoles. She smoothed down the front of her top as if she could smooth away the nerves that danced inside her, as she turned to face her sisters when they marched into the room, voices raised.

'What the hell is going on?'

'Who on God's green earth is Cormac Blake?'

'More importantly, is he hot? Oh!' Alexi stopped in her tracks as Cormac stood up to greet them. 'He *is*.' Alexi's striking blue eyes roved freely over Cormac's body in his tight white t-shirt and thigh-hugging jeans. Victoria felt the urge to go and stand between them, to block her sister's hungry gaze from gobbling up the man *she* was to marry.

'My, my, Victoria,' Alexi purred as she moved towards Cormac slowly, like a tiger stalking its prey. A salacious smile curved her perfectly painted red lips. 'You have picked a handsome prince to save you.'

Victoria rolled her eyes at her sister's antics, but still stepped up beside Cormac.

'Lovely for you to all drop by,' she said, her voice dripping with sarcasm. 'Why don't we take a seat and I'll have tea brought in.'

'I haven't time for tea,' Hattie said, glaring at Cormac from the corner of her eye as she faced her sister. 'I just want to know—'

'Maybe we could talk alone?' Pippa interjected, glowering at her younger sister to shut up, before her eyes darted towards Cormac.

'Anything you say to me, you can say in front of Cormac,' Victoria said with a sniff as she took a seat on the end of the couch, right next to the chair Cormac had been sitting in while they'd waited for the trio. Her sisters took their seats and Cormac slowly sat back in his chair. '*Especially* as we both want to know *how* the hell you know about him.'

'How we know?' Hattie repeated in disbelief. 'How we *know*? How about, why did we find out you're getting married through your bloody official announcement?'

'What?' Victoria spluttered.

'Beg your pardon?' Cormac asked at the same time.

'God, Victoria,' Alexi pipped up as she began to fan herself. 'That voice of his.'

'He is a *person*, Alexi' Victoria ground out through clenched teeth. 'And is sat right here and can *hear you!*'

'Lady Henrietta,' Cormac said carefully. His eyes fixed on Hattie and didn't appear to be giving Alexi the slightest bit of attention. Victoria wanted to smile widely, but kept her face stoic as she turned her attention back to Hattie, who was carefully assessing Cormac.

'I don't go by my title. Henrietta is fine.' It was a start, Victoria conceded.

'Apologies, Henrietta. What did you mean when you said *announcement?*'

'Victoria, Cormac,' Pippa said, pushing what appeared to be even thicker glasses than when Victoria had last seen her up her nose. 'Are you, or are you not, officially betrothed?'

Cormac reached across the gap between the two of them

for her hand, which she gave willingly. He gently squeezed her fingers in support as she raised her chin highly and said, 'We are to be married on the twenty-ninth of August.'

'Yes!' Alexi cried as she jumped to her feet and pumped the air. 'You go, girl!'

'Where... When... Just... *How* did the two of you meet?' Hattie asked.

Victoria glanced towards Cormac; she'd really wanted to have a talk with him before meeting her sisters to give him a good overall picture of them. He had no idea of the minefield he was navigating.

'Cormac was the one who saved me from Simon,' Victoria told them.

'That was, what? Two weeks ago,' Hattie pointed out.

'Twelve days,' Cormac said, making Hattie throw her hands up in the air.

'It's *romantic*,' Alexi counted, glaring at Hattie as she took her seat again. She threw her jeans-clad legs over the arm of the chair as she settled in and pulled out her phone. 'Stop being a bitch. *Victoria* will get the money, not grandfather.'

'It's not *that*,' Hattie countered, her fingers curling up into fists on her knees as she leaned slightly forward. 'But I find it *very* convenient that he just *happened* to save Victoria, whisk her off her feet *and* ask her to marry him in less than a fortnight.'

Victoria sighed and rolled her eyes before explaining the situation.

'...So, Cormac agreed to help me and it's all legal and binding. The announcement wasn't supposed to go out until *Friday*. That's why I messaged each of you yesterday and asked to meet on Wednesday. I was going to tell you before the bloody thing went public.'

The end of her tale was met with silence as her sisters stared at the two of them. Alexi was the only one of the three not gazing back in horror. Instead, her mouth split wide with a delighted smile as she continued to stare at Cormac like he was an all-you-can-eat buffet.

'Oh! *You're* the one from the photos on Saturday!' Alexi finally clicked and returned to her phone, scrolling through whatever it was she had on her screen.

'This is ridiculous!' Hattie continued to protest. 'What the hell do we even know about him?'

'Pretty much everything,' Victoria said, settling into her chair as Cormac's thumb brushed over the top of her fingers. She clung on to him like a lifeline, but she squeezed back as an apology for what she was to say next. 'I wasn't stupid. I had Marcus run a full report.'

'*There*!' Alexi cried triumphantly as she turned her phone around to show the photographs that had caught the three of them out at *The Meat Hut* last week. 'They look so sweet together. But who's the kid?' she asked as she turned it back to glance down at James holding Victoria's hand.

'He's my brother,' Cormac told them. 'James. He's six.'

'Cormac is James' guardian.' Victoria clarified for them. Her three sisters turned their eyes to Cormac, sadness and understanding within them and Victoria knew that each were recalling losing their own mother. Their father hadn't been very hands-on, and Victoria had pretty much taken on the mothering role of Alexi. She'd wanted to help with Hattie, but that had been out of her control. Pippa had been too old to mother, being just two and a half years younger than her. Their sisterly bond had been tried over that period as Victoria focused on Alexi and trying to figure out her own role in life without her mother's support.

'So, you're going to play the role of *stepmother* too.' If Hattie's voice got any higher, dogs would start howling across the city. But she made a valid point. What would her role be with James? To all intents and purposes, Cormac was his father figure and she would be Cormac's wife. But would Cormac want her influence over James in any way? After all, this was a marriage for money, not love, and she had no idea if Cormac planned on sticking around if they were able to have a child—he probably didn't even know yet. But she couldn't let her sisters in on that titbit if they were already outraged by what they'd already heard.

'Well, I...' Victoria turned to Cormac, seeking his help to explain the situation.

'James doesn't call me Dad or anything. He knows he's my brother. He's too smart not to know, and it was easier to do that than tell him lies and try to keep them straight.'

'You're still in the parental role,' Pippa pointed out to him, not unkindly. 'Just because he doesn't call you by a paternal title, doesn't mean you haven't assumed the role of a father or that he doesn't see you in such a position. The same will go for you, Victoria.'

'Victoria,' Hattie sat on the edge of her seat and stared at her, imploring her to listen. And as always, whenever Hattie gave her that look, she knew she wasn't going to like what her sister had to say. 'You have *paid* a man to marry you. A complete and utter stranger—'

'Who saved my life,' Victoria countered.

'Who is a *stripper*—'

'*Was* a male dancer.'

'And are going to have to have sleep with—'

'Like that's going to be a hardship,' Alexi interrupted Hattie this time. Hattie threw up her hands as she stood and walked away in utter frustration.

'Victoria, you have basically got yourself a *prostitute*!' she sneered as she turned on her heel and pointed at Cormac. 'You've paid this poor bloke to shag you in the hopes of getting pregnant—'

'Now that's enough, Hattie!' Pippa shouted, quickly

standing and turning on Hattie as Alexi slammed her hands on her chair and pushed herself up.

'That's not on, Hattie! Take that back!' Alexi cried.

Victoria dropped Cormac's hand as she all but threw herself from her seat and launched herself at her sister. Alexi stepped in Victoria's way, stopping her from reaching Hattie and throttling her.

'Henrietta Constantine Snape! How dare you! How very *dare* you come into my home and start to—'

'Home?' Hattie asked incredulously as she motioned around the room. 'This *isn't* a home, Victoria, it's a hotel.'

'It's our home for now. Until we find something we like. And until then, you will respect us within its wall. Mother would be disgusted by your attitude.'

'Screw you, Tori,' Hattie sneered as she grabbed her things. 'Mummy wouldn't have you do this. Mummy would say the same thing. You've hired a man to fuck you pregnant, and it's disgusting. You've turned him into a whore with your deal and Mummy would be horrified at such a thing! You better ensure Dick doesn't find out—you know how he feels about prostitution—or you'll be making conjugal visits to your husband at Broken Hill.'

The three sisters gasped at Hattie's tirade as they watched her leave in a flurry of curls and twisting fabric.

'Victoria, I'm sure that—'

'She didn't mean—'

'Cormac,' Victoria said, turning back to him. She quickly fell into her seat again, grasping at his hand and searching his face. Her two sisters fell silent immediately. 'What she said isn't true. That's not how this is. It's not what you are, and I don't want you thinking—'

Cormac pulled his hand away from her and rubbed both over his face as he leaned forward, chin in his palms. He looked deep in thought, and Victoria didn't know what to say. She felt her sisters standing across the room, unsure what they should do. She wished they'd go, leave them alone so she could fix this mess before she called Mr Daven up and gave him a good haranguing for messing up and releasing the announcement early.

'But it is true, princess,' Cormac said quietly, holding her gaze. 'No matter how you frame it, you have paid me to marry you and to get you pregnant by *natural* means. Any way you look at it, it is prostitution.'

'My grandfather won't do a *thing*,' she swore to him. She knew the secrets he was hiding thanks to Alistair. She'd use them if she had to and sod her cousin. He'd be King one day, so he had to grow up soon. 'I *promise*. And *I* will never see you in such a light.'

Cormac stared at her before lifting his eyes to glance at both Pippa and Alexi.

'I think I need some time to myself,' he said as he made to stand. She quickly pushed herself up and got out of his way as he left the room.

'Victoria—'

'I'm sorry that—'

'Don't.' She held up her hand to silence the duo. 'I don't want to hear anything from either of you. I'd planned on having an engagement party a week on Friday after the announcement was posted. We have dress fittings this Saturday. Make sure you're available for both. I'll have Kirstie forward you the time.'

They both uttered their agreements and goodbyes before they hurried to leave far quieter than their arrival had been.

Victoria sank down to the couch as her brain replayed everything that had been said between her and Cormac the day she'd propositioned him. The agreement Mr Daven was drawing up for them regarding the financial position. How she'd made assumptions for Cormac in telling him to get rid of his car and forcing a new phone on him. Hell, she'd even given him an allowance, so to speak.

She hadn't called him a prostitute, but she had all the money, all the power over him. The balance was all off kilter in their relationship and until it was level, they'd never be able to move past this.

She picked up the hotel phone and dialled a familiar number.

Before she could go and chase Cormac, she had to ensure she rectified the problem.

～

Cormac had managed to avoid Victoria all afternoon, after the debacle with her sisters, by spending time with James in his room. He'd popped into the bedroom adjoining James' when he'd needed a breather, but he didn't think he'd get away with sleeping there. Not when James would ask questions if he came looking for him. He'd already given Cormac a strange look and asked a *lot* of repetitive questions when Cormac had come in and asked him how to play the game he was enjoying.

Cormac had never particularly liked playing mindless games, but he had to admit, shooting the heads off zombies had been a little therapeutic.

He stood back outside the door he'd been hesitant to enter just twenty-four hours earlier, and once again rested his head against the cool wood as he tried to gather himself together.

Losing the house he'd grown up in had been a tough lesson; his parents had always made life seem so easy, mostly because they'd shielded him from the worst the world could throw at someone. They'd never seemed to scrimp and save, and he'd never seemed to be left wanting for anything. He'd never been spoilt, but he'd had nice things, and he'd just never questioned the way the world went. The fridge was always full, he had new clothes when he needed them, and he never missed out on a school trip.

That was what had hurt the most from learning such a lesson; he wouldn't be able to protect James the way his parents had him. James would know that life was tough and difficult from the get-go. He'd know that money was a struggle, and that the fridge could indeed go bare.

It killed Cormac that he could only get James clothes when he really had worn things to death or completely outgrown them, and then only from charity stores. And it had cut him to the core just a few weeks ago, when he'd found a letter from the school stuffed deep in his little brother's bag for a day trip. James had already learned, having been told *no* so many times before, that he shouldn't even ask. It was the first time Cormac had cried in a long time, as he'd sat there that evening reading the letter and trying to figure out where he could cut a few slivers from the housekeeping budget so James could finally go on a school trip for once, and realised he couldn't make it work.

When he'd first understood the type of life they were going to endure, Cormac had made two rules for himself; number one was James always came first. No matter what, James was his number one priority. The second was he'd never do anything illegal to get by. That if it came to having to commit a crime to keep James, he'd have to say goodbye to his brother.

He pushed the palms of his hands against his eyes as he tried to stop the voices in his head that he'd done it; he'd broken his second rule, and not once but twice. First, he'd agreed to espionage in a round-about sort of way, by telling O'Malley what Victoria had offered, and then he'd become a prostitute. Victoria could pretty it up and try and reassure him she didn't see him that way, but it didn't matter; he was willing to give his body over to her for money.

The thought of O'Malley now knowing about their upcoming nuptials made his stomach drop. He should have stood firm in his refusal to O'Malley, shouldn't have panicked and made that phone call that night. He shouldn't have allowed Mrs Battersea to talk him into changing his mind. After all, two days later, he'd become the world's most expensive gigolo.

He sighed deeply. He'd made some bad decisions in his life that had led him to here, but this time... This time, all he'd done was try and be a good person by stepping in and ensuring Victoria was safe. Wasn't his fault she turned out to be a duchess or whatever. Wasn't his fault his employer was as big a dick bag as the monster who'd attacked Victoria. He shook his head as he pushed the door open, hoping he could push them from his mind at the same time.

'There you are,' Victoria said in a rush of breath as she hurried to him. From the marks in the thick creamy carpet, he could tell she'd been pacing up and down the sitting area. He wondered how long she'd have left it before she came and found him? Would it have been that night? Maybe she'd have sent Merryweather up with breakfast for him in the morning, accepting he needed his space?

'Look. About what Hattie said, you're not... *what* she said.'

Cormac wanted to roll his eyes and tell her to back off. That he still needed space and time to deal with it. But instead, remembering that he was but an employee of hers, he allowed her to take his arm and gently guide him to one of the chairs. He fell into the seat heavily, a sigh punching from him, and tiredness suddenly making him slump. He dropped his head back against the chair and closed his eyes.

'You're not a... *prostitute*,' she whispered the word prostitute as if it was against the law to even utter such a thing.

'You're going to be my *husband*. My partner. The father of my child.'

'Princess, you can give it any other label you want, you still bought and paid for me.' He pointedly ignored the gnaw of guilt deep in the pit of his stomach over why he'd ended up in such a position.

'Please don't call me princess,' she said quietly. Cormac peeked through one eye and saw her casting her gaze downwards as she spoke. 'Not when we're discussing such things.' That was interesting, and he filed it away for later before sighing and sitting up, opening his eyes proper. He reached out and softly cupped her cheek, gently lifting her head so she'd meet his eyes.

'There's nothing to discuss, Victoria. This is what it is. But I'd prefer that no one else knows of our arrangement.'

'No,' Victoria shook her head, pulling herself away from his touch and standing up. 'I won't have you accepting that about yourself. You are *not* that in my eyes. You are my *hero*.' Her voice pleaded with him to understand and accept what she said. 'You're the only good person who has come into my life. The only person who ever did something for me without expecting something, without trying to curry favour or blackmail me.'

The niggle of guilt that had taken up home in his stomach began to devour his insides at the memory of him dropping the coins in the phone box and dialling the digits of O'Malley's number.

'Victoria, please—'

'No!' she said, turning on her heel and grabbing something from the table on the other side of the room. 'You are worth more than you think, more than you put on yourself. I never know who to trust, who I can turn to, but the moment you came into my life, I knew, I just *knew*, that you were someone different.'

Ah hell, she was painting him as a hooker with a heart of gold. Bollocks. She was trying to make him into Julia Roberts in Pretty Woman!

'I knew,' she continued. 'That you were someone I could trust with this!' She thrust the thing in her hand into his face as he stared up at her with tired eyes. It took him a few blinks before he finally glanced down at what she was wiggling under his nose.

A sleek black card danced within her fingers; a wisp of silver decorated one length of it. He slowly sat back and reached for her gift. It was the size of a credit card but made of black metal. The wisp of silver was his name, scrawled in perfect cursive across the bottom of it and four numbers sat beneath. There was nothing else to give him a clue as to what it was. He cast his eyes up at her, as she looked hopeful at him.

'Go on, give me a clue?' he said as he slouched in his seat and twisted the card between his index fingers. 'Does this give me access to another secret floor of this place?' He smiled, but it quickly disappeared when her cheeks flooded with colour and mortification filled her eyes.

'Oh, it's a bank card.' And everything she'd just protested was wiped away as she handed him his pay cheque. He felt bitter disappointment; for just a second, he'd had hope in her words... but he was intrigued by the way the card looked; it wasn't like any he'd seen before.

'This card has an unlimited value. You could walk into a Ferrari dealership in the morning, slap this down and drive out with one there and then.'

He was fairly sure that wasn't exactly true for luxury cars, but he got her meaning. He stared down at the thing, a little impressed.

'When I asked you to marry me, Cormac, it wasn't for sex. I mean I know we have to have it to fulfil the stipulations, but…' She began to play with her necklace again as she searched for the right words, until finally her shoulders slumped when they eluded her.

'Look, I know we agreed a payment for you to marry me, but truly, as my husband, what I have is yours.'

He considered her words. It kind of felt like she was just paying a bigger price tag for his *services*, but he got the sentiment behind it. She was trying, at least.

'Okay, Victoria, I get it, but maybe… Maybe no one else finds out about this, yeah?' She nodded her head vigorously.

'Promise.' She mimed zipping her mouth shut. 'And I've already spoken to my sisters about keeping things private. They've promised not to mention it again.'

'Even Henrietta?' he asked, sceptically. He had a feeling she wanted to shout it from the rooftops. He wasn't completely sure of the story between the two sisters, but he knew there was a rift. Geri had told him of it when she'd been rabbiting on about the Snapes since the moment Victoria had left the club. There were various theories floating about—and he'd heard a few from his friend—but Cormac had a feeling it was more than just jealousy or a fall-out over their differing lives.

'Even Hattie,' she said, solemnly.

'And you're not frightened I'm going to run off with this and bleed you dry before the big day?' he asked, the beginning of a smirk on his lips as he stared up at her. He was about to list a good number of insanely expensive things he could run off and buy, when she licked her lips and shook her head.

'Something inside me tells me I can trust you. That you're probably the only person I really can trust right now.'

The smile fell from his lips as she spoke. She couldn't trust him; he'd already betrayed her trust before she'd even thought she could have it. He rubbed his hand over his face.

This was such a mess. He didn't even know if he had the right to be offended by what Henrietta had said.

'Okay.'

'Okay?' she asked hopefully.

'Yeah, but gimme some time, alright?'

Victoria nodded enthusiastically. 'Okay. But just one thing?'

He sighed. 'Yes?'

'Well, I had a call from the palace… Our engagement party has been moved to Saturday night; do you have some guests you'd like to invite?'

Cormac groaned as he slunk down in his chair and squeezed his eyes closed.

'I am *never* gonna hear the end of this…'

CHAPTER THREE

'And you've been reviewing the files Kirstie sent to you?'

'Yes,' Cormac called back exasperated, as he stood in front of the mirror, frowning at the strip of fabric wrapped around his neck. It didn't look anything like bow ties should. Why the store had insisted he have a real one instead of a clip-on, he didn't know.

How the hell did people do these things? He was supposed to look like James Bond, all suave and sophisticated, not a freaking adorable puppy in a shop window waiting for pats on the head and scratches behind the ear.

'What are you doing?' Victoria asked as she stepped into the dressing room, affixing an earring in her earlobe.

A smile quirked her lips as he faced her, and she saw his "bow tie".

'What *have* you done?' She chuckled, and the warmth within it curled around Cormac's insides, turning him to mush. They'd been tiptoeing around one another all week, being polite and courteous at all times. She was waiting for him to indicate to her that everything was okay between them again, that they could begin to build something of a relationship—be it friendship or something more—and move on with their lives. And Cormac ached to bridge the gap between them, to fix whatever was broken, but he had a feeling it wasn't something *between them* that needed fixing—it was *him*.

He'd been wrestling with his conscience, wondering if he should tell Victoria what he'd done, but while the reasonable voice within him kept saying *yes, she'll understand*, the other voice—that sounded even more reasonable—questioned *why?*

It was over and done with. He hadn't actually betrayed her, and it wasn't as if he was ever going to have anything to do with O'Malley again.

He offered his own lopsided smile as she came over to him.

She raised her hand slowly towards him, giving him the chance to lean back and pull away if he wanted. Instead, he stood fast, and her elegant fingers gently tugged at the bow to unravel it.

'I'm guessing you've never worn one of these before?' She undid the knot from under his bow and began to untwist the lengths. He shook his head.

'When my mum hired my tux for our formal dance at school, she got me one that was already done and just fastened around my neck with a clip.' Victoria tutted at the confession as she began to fix the mess he'd made. 'I'm pretty useless with things like this; can't do anything fancier than a simple knot in a tie either. Luckily, James' school tie is elasticated.'

'He'll have to wear a proper one at Highbourne,' she told him as she made the bow before slipping the other side under and over the back of it. 'They insist on a Windsor knot there.' Cormac groaned. 'Hey! At least it's not something ridiculously complicated like an Eldredge or a Van Wijk. Although, the Trinity knot always seems to catch my eye. I think it's the way it looks; it's quite hypnotic. There,' she said as she pulled the tie tight. She rested her hands lightly against his chest and tilted her head one way, then the other as she took in her handiwork.

She licked her perfect red lips before glancing up at him through her long dark lashes. 'Perfect,' she purred.

She was, he agreed, as he nodded his head along with her own. He reached up to touch the tie and brushed her fingers with his as he brought it away again. He watched the sudden rise and fall of her chest as she took in a shaky breath at their contact.

Why couldn't he just reach down and kiss her? Why couldn't he just get over this stupidity he seemed to be suffering?

'James will be waiting,' she whispered as she ran her fingers down the lapels of his jacket, making sure they were symmetrical. 'But don't worry,' she told him with a far too bright grin. 'He's got a clip on.'

Cormac watched her leave and cursed himself again.

∼

Cormac stared out of the window overlooking the immaculate gardens as the partygoers mingled behind him. He pulled at his tie for the millionth time, the feeling it was choking him not going away, when another hand slapped at his.

'What the—'

'Stop fidgeting,' Geri said as she scowled up at him. Cormac couldn't help the smile that spread over his face at his blue-haired friend. 'You look like a film star,' she told him casually before taking a long sip of her colourful drink through a straw.

She stared at him through ultra-long bright blue false eyelashes. She was wearing her black contacts tonight, and it looked rather perturbing, but he figured that was what she was going for. She wore the most feminine dress he'd ever seen her in; an all-black floor-length, skin-tight number, decorated with beads and lace all. Really classy.

'When did you get here?' he asked. 'Did you come with the guys?' He peered over her head, looking for his other three invitees. Victoria had told him he could invite as many people as he wanted, but he'd struggled to think of anyone other than Geri.

He'd considered Axel, Harry, and Nick, thinking he could probably trust them not to go and sell their stories to the media, but he hadn't been sure if he was close enough to them to ask them to such an event. Finally, he'd caved; he hadn't wanted to look utterly pathetic with only *one* guest on the list. Victoria had ensured she'd kept her numbers down, her closest friends and her family—who were all total arseholes, he decided as he glanced over the heads of everyone for his friends.

'Why Geri, you look lovely!' Geri said. 'Where did you get that dress you spent two months wages on just for *my* little engagement party that I totally forgot to tell you about? I'm so sorry you had to find out about it only when some fancy-ass, weirdly dressed dude showed up at your door. Oh, and I'm also sorry I never called to even *tell* you I was engaged to a woman I only just met and—'

'Okay, Geri,' Cormac interrupted, taking her elbow lightly in his hand and steering her even further away from the crowd behind her. 'I'm sorry.'

'Sorry?' She looked wholly unimpressed and quickly shook his hand away. He'd forgotten her no-touching rule.

'Yes, I'm sorry. I meant to call, but I don't have your number.'

'Cormac, we all know you *don't* do phones,' she replied with an eye-roll.

He smirked down at her before reaching into his inside pocket and pulling out the shiny black phone just enough for her to be able to see it.

'Well, as I live and breathe!' she said in quiet surprise as her eyes fell on the device. 'You've finally stepped into the twenty-first century. Gimme!' She made grabby hands towards it and with a sigh, he handed it over to her, knowing it was easier to just do it than argue. She huffed an annoyed breath before pinning him with an unimpressed glare through her long fringe.

'You *need* a password on this,' she whispered so no one else could overhear, before dropping her gaze back to the device in her hand and began tapping away. 'There, now you have my number and'—she pressed the call button and allowed the line to connect with one ring before hanging up—'now I have yours. There's no escaping me now, Cormac Blake! I want regular updates on how the other half live.' She held the phone back out to him. Cormac glanced at the tiny bag at the end of a chain over her shoulder.

'How'd you fit your phone in that? No, wait, I don't want to know where you've stashed it.'

'Ha, ha,' she said dryly. 'You told us not to bring them. Your guy who made us sign the NDA before we even got to touch the posh envelope said it was so we can't sell any pictures or recordings'—Cormac's brows rose in surprise—'which is annoying as I figured the least you could do was let me take a few snaps of you and Lady Snape together.' She eyed him speculatively before adding. 'You know, I'd be able to buy one of those cute beach cottages up on Wessex Shores if I told them how the two of you *actually* met.'

'Don't you *dare!*' he snarled, an instinctive response as he recalled that night with perfect clarity. Geri instantly held up her hands in surrender.

'Down, big boy. One, I was joking, and two, do you really think *I'd* want to be in the papers? Anonymous or not?'

He knew she was telling the truth; she gobbled up the gossip rags like they were going out of fashion, but she did say that anyone who went to them to spread those kind of things deserved to be squished under a perfectly sparkling stiletto shoe of the socialites, heirs and heiresses, and anyone else they betrayed.

'Not funny, Ger.'

'What's not funny? Prince Artie's tuxedo? Because trust me, it's *hilarious*,' Harry said as he joined the duo. 'He's acting like it's some fabulous new thing with the way he's courting compliments. Bitch, please. It's a two-year-old Ralph Lauren, and anyone who's *anyone* knows it. Deval Vine is winding him up over it, and he doesn't even realise.'

'Deval Vine is here?' Geri said, instantly standing on her tiptoes and craning her neck to try and see over the crowd. 'Axel, lift me up.'

'No!' Cormac hissed as the giant bouncer—who looked more like the incredible hulk squished into formal attire—reached down to pick her up. The man stood like a deer caught in headlights as he stared at Cormac with his hands on Geri's hips. 'Just behave, everyone, like *normal* people.'

'Bitch, we *are* normal,' Harry scoffed. 'It's this lot that aren't.'

The group considered his words as they gazed out towards the party guests.

'I have no idea who Deval Vine is,' Cormac admitted, breaking the silence that had descended over them. He grabbed the glass of whisky from the waiter who brought over his drink and downed the amber liquid in one gulp before putting it back and asking for another—this time a double.

'He's only the editor of *Chic* magazine,' Geri told him.

'*The* magazine of the fashion world,' Harry said as he grabbed a weird-looking piece of food from a different waiter's tray.

'Why would Victoria invite him?' he asked, glancing around the room to see if he could spot Prince Arthur. He'd made a point of learning who Victoria's cousins were, just to be able to avoid the ones she'd desperately insisted on. Arthur—or Artie as he'd been known by the public since he was a baby—was number one on that list.

'Um, maybe because you have an interview coming up with the magazine...' Geri glanced towards Harry who stared back at her agog at Cormac's absent-mindedness. 'You know, *before* the wedding.'

'We're doing interviews?'

Geri blinked rapidly as she processed his words, while Harry shook his head, mouth hanging open;

'Since it started in 1892, *Chic* has interviewed every royal couple before their big day,' Axel told him. 'They're also the ones who always get the rights to the wedding photos when they're ready to be released. What?' he asked as all eyes turned to him. 'I know stuff. Just because I throw people out on their arses don't mean I can't appreciate nice things.'

'We are going to have to have a talk. *Soon*,' Harry told the giant, before turning back to Cormac with a *really, Axel knows this shit and you don't?* look on his face. At least, that was what Cormac took from the expression the other man gave him. Cormac dropped his head back between his shoulders and made an exasperated groan.

'There's so much to learn. My head is going to explode.'

'Just do what I do,' Nick finally spoke up. 'Just smile and

nod when people tell you things. Then you don't have to remember because they just think that you agree with them.'

'That's... Yeah, anyway,' Geri said, turning back to Cormac, but he thought Nick might have something there. 'Have you met any of the royals?' She glanced around her and Cormac knew she was looking for an introduction.

'I've met Victoria's sisters,' he said with a shrug. 'But this lot, nah. Victoria said to stay away from them for as long as I could, and so far, none of them have done anything other than cast me side-eye, so we're all golden.'

'Wait, *none* of them?' Now it was Harry who looked perplexed. 'Not a single one of them has come over to actually speak to the man who just magically popped up into Lady Snape's life?'

Cormac shook his head. 'Nah, Victoria reckons they're pissed at me, because now it means they can all be married off by King Richard. That means no more of the carefree good life. Instead, it's babies and titles and more responsibilities.'

'Oh, yeah,' Geri said, scanning the room again. 'I'll bet Alistair will be next.'

'Ugh, please don't say that,' said a new voice. The group turned as one to see His Royal Highness, Prince Alistair of Avalone, standing just at Cormac's left shoulder, peering into the group. A collective gasp sounded before a flurry of motion kicked into them all; the men dipping in bows, while Geri tried to curtsey in the tight dress she wore.

'Oh, no, don't do that,' Alistair said quickly, motioning for them to stand up. 'Not here, not in front of all my cousins; it'll only give them more ammunition.'

'Ammunition?' Harry asked, while Nick smiled and nodded along. Cormac rolled his eyes.

'Yes,' Alistair said forlornly as he glanced out at the rest of the room. 'You try being the thing between them and the Crown and see how well you stand up.'

Nick nodded again before wincing as Geri shoved her elbow into his side.

'Your Royal Highness—' she began.

'Please, call me Alistair. I mean, Cormac here is going to be family soon, and you're all his friends, so...'

This time, everyone seemed to do a Nick as they smiled and nodded. Cormac made to speak when a fanfare sounded, scaring the shit out of him. He wasn't the only one in the group to jump. All his friends did the same, but Alistair merely groaned, dropping his head back to stare at the ceiling before focusing his attention on the doors at the other end of the room. The group followed suit.

'Their Royal Majesties, King Richard and Queen Katrine of Avalone,' the herald announced to the room. The beginning notes of the national anthem began to play from the string quartet in the corner, as the doors to the ballroom swung open. A small silver-haired man strode into the room, one hand shoved deep into his pocket, with his diminutive queen at his side.

'They say he has one hand smaller than the other,' Geri whispered to Cormac. 'That it was affected by polio as a child or something.'

'You're half right. It's actually caused by Poland's Syndrome,' Alistair hissed behind Cormac's back to the blue-haired wonder. 'By the way, I *love* your hair.'

Cormac heard Geri giggle, and he knocked her with his elbow to get her to shut up.

The *King* of Avalone was here. The fucking *King*! He was going to meet him. Victoria had said it would be tonight, but he hadn't really understood what that meant until now, with all these people standing around with hands on hearts as they sang the anthem of their nation, of their Royal Family.

'Are you okay?' Alistair asked, genuinely concerned. 'You've gone a little pale.'

'I gotta meet the King,' he breathed. Alistair seemed to understand as he merely responded with an *ah*, to his dilemma.

'He's not too bad.' Cormac glanced at the prince from the corner of his eye. 'Okay,' Alistair relented 'Just learn to blend into the background. It's what Victoria and her sisters try and do. It seems to work for them.'

'Not an option for you?' Harry asked, his curiosity piqued.

'Not when you're in direct line to the throne.'

'And how the hell am *I* supposed to do that when it's *my* engagement party?' Cormac asked. Geri's hand slapped his again as he reached up to tug at his bow tie, but no one gave him an answer.

When the anthem finished, they all began a round of applause and Victoria suddenly appeared in front of the King, dipping into a curtsey so deep Cormac didn't think it was good for her knees. She seemed to hold it forever, and he frowned, wondering why the King wasn't letting her up.

'Oh, shit!' Cormac said, thrusting his glass at Alistair. 'I'm supposed to be over there too.'

'Good luck!' his new royal friend called, raising Cormac's untouched drink his way as he tried to quickly manoeuvre through the crowd, who smirked at him as he went.

He reached the King and Queen and took a deep breath before bowing from the waist and holding a perfect forty-five degree angle as dictated by royal tradition.

He heard the frustrated sigh the King heaved.

'Arise.' With no names or acknowledgement beyond that single word, Cormac knew that he'd royally screwed up. Cormac stood back to his full height and looked down at the King; the man must have only stood about five foot five, but it was Cormac who felt tiny when his cold blue eyes stared at him.

'Victoria, I will speak with you.' The monarch didn't take his eyes from Cormac, but Cormac saw her head bob before she stepped aside. Unsure of what to do, the King passed him, his eyes still on Cormac's until it was physically impossible to hold them any longer. But even knowing the King was walking away, Cormac couldn't help but feel as if the monarch was still watching him.

He heard a door open, before closing almost immediately after.

Alistair came up to him and handed him back his drink.

'Deep breath, buddy,' the other man said, and Cormac found himself doing exactly that, oblivious to the point he'd been holding it the whole time. 'Knock this back and then get another. I'll see you in a while. Duty calls.' The man patted his shoulder before following in the direction of his grandfather.

Cormac followed Alistair's instructions, grabbing another drink from the waiting staff who had begun to move around the party again as their guests began to murmur; obviously, the topic of conversation was how much of a disaster that had been.

'I've seen worse,' Queen Katrine said with an amused grin before someone caught her attention and she wandered away.

'Cormac, are you okay?' Geri asked, taking the again empty tumbler from him, and replacing it with another. The waiter went to protest, but Geri's glare made the man scarper away.

'Probably shouldn't give him too many of those if he's got to face the King again,' Axel reminded them. Cormac closed his eyes and swallowed the drink in one gulp.

Victoria followed her grandfather into the throne room and took a deep breath as she positioned herself at the bottom of the dais. She'd been expecting to be called before him since the official announcement was released, figured he'd demand to speak to her when she called the palace to ask to use the Blue Ballroom—the smallest of the three in the palace—but Michael, the palace's head butler, had merely told her it would be arranged.

She had hoped against hope that the King was merely going to ignore her pending nuptials as anything other than finally being done with her and being able to get Alistair down the aisle next. In fact, she'd counted on him reading her announcement and immediately calling Alistair with the date of his own wedding.

She really should have known better, she realised, as she watched him take a seat on his throne. He was so bloody dramatic. She heard the door open and close again and caught Alistair coming in from the corner of her eye. At least the Grand Duke wasn't—

Victoria took another deep breath and resisted rolling her eyes as her uncle followed in her cousin's wake.

Of bloody course. He just *loved* seeing her or her sisters being taken to task. Victoria swore he held a grudge against them just because her mother ran off and forced his father to marry him off immediately to beat her mother's elopement by one day—officially. She bit back the smirk, recalling her mother showing her their true marriage announcement dated one day before the Grand Duke's.

'Lady Snape.' King Richard's voice, as husky and thready as it had once been deep and commanding, called her to attention.

'Your Majesty,' she curtseyed again, this time shallow and quick.

'I think you know why I wish to speak to you.'

'You wish to congratulate me on my betrothal and discuss my upcoming wedding plans?' Her hopes were dashed when her grandfather narrowed his eyes and pursed his lips.

'We'll get to that. Maybe.' Victoria swallowed. 'Would you care to explain to me the reason for the expedience of your engagement?'

'When one falls in love, one knows, sire.'

She tried to keep her tone casual, almost flippant and managed not to shrug as she spoke. Richard shook his head at her antics before dropping his cheek into his hand as he watched her. 'There's no point in waiting when one knows.'

'You are most *certainly* your mother's child,' he muttered. Victoria swelled with pride at the comment, uncaring if it was meant to be a slight against her. They all knew her mother had barely been tolerated after her elopement.

'Exactly, and she knew when she fell in love.'

She bit her lip and dipped her head a little, a slight hesitation before she added, 'I imagine the Grand Duke did too, with how suddenly his wedding occurred—'

'You bite your tongue, girl!' her uncle snarled from somewhere behind her. Richard held up his other hand as he kept his gaze on her. She heard the door open and close again in the silence and she felt a little smug in the fact her uncle had been dismissed from her berating. She wished she were brave enough to land a few more points that evening.

Finally, the King sighed. 'Pray tell,' he began. 'How did you meet your fiancé?'

Victoria's mind whirled as she tried to figure out how much he knew. Marcus said he'd intercepted Geri's call the night of the attack, but then the papers had printed that picture of her stepping out of the club and, afterwards, the hospital. She'd been waiting for the King's call about that ever since, but it had never arrived.

The same with him not calling her after the announcement had appeared.

A flicker of hope sparked to life at the thought that perhaps he didn't know anything, and she'd be able to play this off as simply falling in love and not wanting to wait after all.

He shifted in his seat, straightening up, his fingers curling over the front of the arms of his throne as if he wanted to dig his nails in. Victoria swallowed; he wasn't known for being temperate when he wanted something. When he spoke, his tone was impatient, the words spoken through clenched teeth.

'I am waiting.'

She opened her mouth to speak, to spin her tale, but she caught Marcus' warning a second before she spoke. He stood to her grandfather's right, just off the dais, and while he didn't move, his eyes stared intensely at her, and his face—while anyone else would say it remained neutral—told Victoria not to try and bullshit the King. The story they were going to tell the press about their whirlwind romance would not work here.

'I met him after a date went wrong and Cormac came to my rescue.' It was the truth, just worded a little less dramatically than it had been.

'That's an interesting way of explaining how you were drugged, possibly to be sexually assaulted, avoided being kidnapped only by happenstance, ended up in a *strip* club, and are now *engaged* to the *stripper* who rescued you—as you put it.' He screamed the word *stripper* before going deathly quiet again. Victoria turned accusing eyes towards Marcus, but the man remained stoic even to her.

'I wouldn't look to Captain Walker,' Richard said, calling

her attention back on him. 'The captain here might still be soft towards you, might hold things from me that I *should* know about, but he's the captain of *my* guard, *not* the police force as much as he, his predecessors, and I'm sure his successors would like to think. Nor does he control the judges; those at the Broken Hill report directly to me.'

She bit her lip, unsure of what she was supposed to say.

She wasn't sure if he was angrier at the fact she'd been attacked, that it had been dealt with without him, that they had attempted to hide it from him completely, or that she'd rushed into an engagement.

It was probably all the above.

She was also sure that he hadn't been too happy at the whole dating spree she'd been on just months before she announced a surprise engagement on him and the nation.

But she didn't want him knowing about the will, didn't want him to hinder her sisters in their plight of getting their own inheritances—even if they didn't seem that interested in the money—just so he could exact revenge on their father. Even in death, she knew their grandfather wouldn't hold back on his vengeance.

He blamed Patrick Snape for so many transgressions when really he should have been looking in the mirror, as her mother had told her not long before she'd died and Victoria could finally begin to understand the goings on that their family kept secret from the public. Of course, she couldn't say such things to her grandfather.

'Cat finally got your tongue?'

'Yes, all those things happened,' she finally admitted, deciding a half-truth was better than any other option she had. 'As I said, I met Cormac when he rescued me from a date that went wrong. I spoke nothing but the truth.' The King scoffed at her audacity.

'So, you're going to marry a man you just met last week-'

'Seventeen days ago,' she interrupted. Marcus actively rolled his eyes, and she heard Alistair groan somewhere behind her.

Richard merely glared at her with his cold, piercing blue eyes.

It wasn't like her. Victoria was the one who kept her head down, who blended in, who kept her mouth shut in the presence of the man before her, speaking only when spoken to. Sure, she'd been taken to task before, but it had always been for little, insignificant reasons.

But, she decided, in for a bit, in for a crown, and ploughed on—she'd probably never get the chance again!

'And yes, I *am* going to marry him. As you are aware, the date is set for August twenty-ninth, the Archbishop of Avon will preside over the service at the Cathedral, and invites are already being printed and will be sent next week.'

'I will remind you this once'—Richard held up a single finger—'that you will speak only when spoken to.'

'My apologies, Your *Majesty*, but I'm simply unsure which one of my supposed transgressions offends you the most,' she snapped back. Marcus shook his head in exasperation at her, as the King shot up out of his chair, moving so quickly for someone who appeared so old and frail. However, Victoria knew that fragility to be an act, something to keep the public soft and caring towards him. The man was as fit as he'd ever been and as sharp as a knife ready to plunge into you with deadly force.

She heard heated whispering behind her but resisted the urge to turn away from her grandfather to glare at the spectators so obviously enjoying the show.

'There is a man sitting in the Broken Hill serving a minimum of thirty years. I'd like to know *why* you felt it important to not bring this to the public's attention.'

'I didn't want the public to know that I had been vulnerable. If it was in the public domain that someone was able to do such a thing to a member of their Royal Family, there might be an outcry. My aunts, uncles, cousins, and sisters could all be shut away in fear, and as it was an error in my judgement—trusting a sister's word over getting a full security debrief from Captain Walker—I decided not to subject my family to such measures. Again.'

King Richard narrowed his eyes at her. She knew it was the perfect *diplomatic* answer. It was also completely true. No one outside of the royal circle would know that Victoria would need both hands and three toes to count how many thwarted kidnapping attempts she'd endured before she'd even hit thirty. She'd had four stalkers, had been hacked seven times, and had even been held hostage once. Although, that was more a case of wrong place, wrong time than a deliberate means of getting to her, and the public had *definitely* been aware of that one. Hell, part of it had been broadcast live on the internet. And afterwards, the whole family had been locked down for months before they slowly started to begin public appearances again after the Guard established they had caught everyone involved in the situation.

'Yet you are quite happy to have your love life in the public domain? You've made quite a little spectacle of yourself these last few months. Different man on your arm every time you go out-'

Something within Victoria snapped. She was so tired of being pushed around, of being quiet, trying to be the perfect wallflower so she never drew attention to herself. Where had all that got her? A broken heart, problematic relationships with her sisters, and an empty life. She wanted a quiet, happy life, where she could welcome her sisters and forge relationships with them, the relationships she should have always had. She wanted a happy marriage and children running around a home. She wanted to *watch* royal events, not be part of them, and she wanted, so desperately wanted, not to be beholden to the man standing in front of her any longer!

'No! No, I'm not happy to have my life splashed over the media! I don't *want* the public knowing every facet of my *life*. I am not a source of gossip or entertainment. I should be able to go for a lunch with a friend or loved one without having my every move scrutinised; what did I eat and drink, who was I with, what did they have? It's infuriating!'

She understood people who sought fame; actors, singers, influencers—whatever the hell they were!—being hounded and tracked, since it was what they *needed* to stay relevant. But people like her who had no choice in this; who were *born* into a family that had already established themselves as a public entity, why was *she* subjected to such scrutiny?

'*You* are infuriating. You are a member of the Royal Family; you are privileged in ways so many others are not-'

'I don't *want* to be a member of the Royal Family!' she shouted back. 'I want out! Once I am married, it will be over and done with. I will rescind my title, give up my patronages —I've already moved out of Renfrew.'

'How dare you speak to me-'

He moved his hand, raising his fist towards her and Victoria knew she was going to get the finger in the face, the old index jabbing towards her when he wanted to make a point. She always found it hard to focus on him when he did that, no matter how hard she tried. She always ended up looking at the finger and going cross-eyed in the process. It meant she'd lose the argument due to losing the fire in her belly, and once more, he'd beat her into submission.

Damn him.

'Don't you dare!' roared a voice behind her, accompanied by heavy rushing footsteps. It took a moment for both her and the King to realise someone had interrupted them, but not for Marcus or the rest of the Guard present. And it took another second for Victoria to recognise who was causing the commotion.

'Cormac!' Alistair shouted out after her betrothed, but was too late. Victoria turned just in time to see two Royal Protection Officers trying to tackle Cormac to the floor, grappling with him as he fought them off. He kicked one away with a move she'd only seen in movies, and then blocked the other with his shoulder. He used that guard as an aid to kick at another one, before grabbing the same officer's arm and twisting it around. The first Guard came back at him, and Cormac punched him square in the nose, making it explode blood across his face.

Victoria gasped at the action, her hand flying to her mouth in both horror and awe. She'd never seen the officers have such a hard time in dealing with a single attacker, and she was caught up in admiring her Prince Charming—who, dressed in a tuxedo, looked more like James Bond—that it took her longer than it should have to react.

'Get off him!' she cried as she hurried forward, only to have another Guard hold her back. Marcus and two more Guards joined the fray and finally, they caught him, dropping him to the floor. Marcus planted his knee between Cormac's shoulder blades as one officer sat on his feet and the other kept his arms behind his back. Cormac struggled, trying to twist from their grasp but they held him firm. She tried to dart past the Guard blocking her, but he grabbed her around the middle and lifted her off her feet as she kicked out and scrambled blindly at his hands.

'Get off him!' she screamed as she thrashed as much as she could.

'Put her down!' Cormac grunted; his voice not as strong as it had been. He kept trying to lift his head to see where she was, and what was happening to her, but Marcus kept forcing his knee further into Cormac's back, making it difficult for her betrothed to lift his head for too long.

'Marcus, stop it!' she cried. She dug her nails into the underside of the wrists of her captor—just as Marcus had shown her—and the man barked out a cry of pain, trying to keep his grip on her as she dug deeper still. She swore she drew blood before the Guard was no longer able to keep his grasp on her, and she finally found her feet touching the ground again and ran to Cormac's side.

'Get off him,' she snarled as she pushed at Marcus. He refused to move, and she didn't have the strength to force him off her future husband.

She dropped to the floor and allowed Cormac to see that she was okay, relatively unharmed, and begged that he calm down.

'Please, they won't let you go if you keep raging like this,' she told him, trying to keep her voice as calm as possible.

'Get them off me! I won't have them treat you like that!'

'But why did you get riled up?' she asked, not having the slightest what had sparked her perpetual rescuer to come once more charging in on his white steed. There'd been nothing out of the usual in the meeting and she hadn't even known Cormac was in the room.

'He was going to hit you,' Cormac spat and moved his head to try and glare at the King who stood a few steps away, staring down at the duo with open curiosity.

'Oh please,' her uncle said. 'No one was going to hit anyone. I don't know where *you* come from but in polite-'

'This has nothing to do with you,' she sneered at her uncle.

'I will be King one day, so this has-'

'Yeah, well, you're not at the moment are you!'

'Father,' Alistair said quietly at his side. 'Perhaps now isn't the best time to-'

'Don't be so impertinent, boy!' the Grand Duke snapped back, silencing Alistair.

Her cousin bowed his head and stepped away from the scene, keeping his eyes focused on what was before him. If she hadn't been so distressed, Victoria would have seen the embarrassment and humiliation that tinged Alistair's cheeks, and the anger and defiance in his eyes.

'Listen to your son, Harold,' Richard murmured, silencing the other man before he could speak again.

'Can you please let him go?' she begged Marcus as she continued to stroke Cormac's short, dark-blond hair, desperately trying to get him to calm down. 'Please? He won't go for anyone, I promise. Will you?'

'I will if they raise their hand to you again!' he spat, before grunting as Marcus pressed his knee down again.

'But they won't,' she said, trying to soothe him. 'No one here ever has, and they never will.'

'But *he* was going to!' He stared at King Richard with open hostility and suddenly the pieces fell into place. He'd thought her grandfather was going to hit her when he'd been about to do his patented finger wag. She didn't know whether to laugh or cry.

'Let him up,' the King's voice commanded and immediately, the guards released Cormac. He groaned as his limbs were freed, but he heaved himself to his knees and Victoria threw her arms around him, hugging him close. She felt him return it briefly before he gently untangled himself from her arms and rose to his feet, holding out his hand for her to follow suit.

'You might be the King,' Cormac growled, glaring down at the ageing monarch as he wrapped his arm around Victoria's waist and held her close to his side. 'But if you ever raise a hand to her again, I promise you, I will break it.'

King Richard said nothing, but Victoria reached up and gently turned Cormac's face towards her.

'Cormac, he wasn't going to hit me, he does this thing'—she glanced towards her grandfather from the corner of her eye—'where he wags his finger at us when he's *really* angry. It gets right up close to you, often making your eyes go squiffy as you look at it, but that's it. That's what he was going to do.'

Cormac frowned in confusion at her before looking at the King and then towards Alistair, who nodded his head quickly.

'We've all been on the end of it,' the prince told Cormac with a shrug. 'It's a bit of an in-joke between all us grandchildren. If we don't get the finger, we clearly weren't bad enough. Must try harder next time and all that. We even have a scoreboard of who's got the most finger wags. Artie and Franny are currently tied, but Franny believes—'

Ahem! The King cleared his throat as he stared at his future replacement in consternation.

'I mean...' Alistair stopped talking and bowed to his grandfather before he turned and stepped over to where he'd been observing earlier. The Grand Duke sighed heavily but said nothing.

'You're a stripper.' It wasn't a question.

'He *was*,' Victoria interjected.

'I wasn't speaking to you. You had your chance to tell me the truth and you didn't.' King Richard didn't even look at her as he spoke. His blue eyes focused on Cormac who kept his green ones on the smaller man. 'I will say again, you're a *stripper*.'

'I was,' Cormac repeated Victoria's words. 'Victoria asked me to give it up, so I did.'

'I'll bet she did. In return for a good lifestyle that she'll be paying for.'

Cormac shrugged. 'I have a six-year-old brother to take

care of. Continue stripping and struggling with debt, and potentially lose my brother, *or* marry an amazing, beautiful woman, who wants nothing more than to elevate us out of all the crap we endure? I think I'll take the second option.'

Victoria couldn't help the smile as he described her as *amazing* and *beautiful*. She shifted against him and he glanced down to her.

'You really think I'm beautiful?' she asked, her voice husky with shyness at her family being witnesses to their little moment. Cormac's hand reached up and brushed behind her ear what had been perfect curls before she'd been hauled off her feet.

'The most beautiful woman I've ever seen.'

There was such conviction in his eyes, it took Victoria's breath away. She sighed dreamily, feeling exactly like the women in Alexi's trashy romance novels—not that *she'd* ever read them—when the hero declared his love for the heroine. Of course, she was no heroine and Cormac was certainly not declaring his love for her, but she suddenly knew she wanted it. She wanted this man to be the real deal, to truly be a prince in disguise. She wanted him to sweep her off her feet and love her with all his heart and she wanted to love him in return. Truly, madly, and deeply.

He must have seen something within her gaze as his eyes slipped to her lips and she couldn't help but sweep her tongue over them, inviting him to take a taste.

His mouth lifted into a half smile, and his head lowered slightly, but instead of brushing her mouth with his, he dropped his lips to her ear and a pleasurable shiver trembled through her body as he whispered, 'I'm kissing you tonight, princess.'

Oh, God! Her body almost vibrated at the words. He'd promised that when the time came to kiss her, he wouldn't stop. The image of the two of them entwined on her bed began to form in her mind—

'I don't want this getting out, about him being a stripper, Victoria.'

This time, Victoria's sigh was one of frustration as her grandfather rudely interrupted her daydreams and completely banished the warm fuzzy feeling she'd had going on inside her chest.

'I can't stop it getting out there,' she said, putting a little bit of distance between her and Cormac but refusing to let go of him, despite it being improper. 'But it's not something we're going to advertise.'

'I assume you have a cover story to tell the world?'

'Of course. I can have Kirstie send you a copy.'

'I want it before the end of the party. And *I* will ensure that it doesn't get out there.' And with that, Victoria knew she had been dismissed. She turned, dropping her hand from Cormac's waist to take his hand in hers when the King stopped them again.

'Just one more thing, Mr Blake. Where did you learn to fight like that?' Richard asked, his blue eyes scrutinising the younger man.

'Um, I took part in mixed martial arts, junior division.'

'*Junior?*'

Cormac looked down at where his fingers were entwined with hers and she knew he didn't want to explain any further. Thankfully, her grandfather took the hint.

'You'll have been out of that for how many years?'

'Um, six-ish?'

'And yet you can still fight like that?'

Cormac shrugged. 'I didn't really think about it. I still do stuff at the gym to keep in shape—that was just muscle memory, I guess.'

'Well, I must say, at least I know my granddaughter will

be safe having you around. Have a good evening.' And with that the guardsmen stepped away and moved with the King towards the doors at the opposite side of the throne room from the ones that led to the party, leaving them, Alastair, and Grand Duke Harold remaining.

Victoria blinked at the door her grandfather had disappeared through. Had he just... Did he somewhat *approve* of Cormac for *fighting* his protection detail? Or was it more for trying to protect her?

'Are you okay?' Cormac asked in her ear, causing her to stare up at him dazedly.

'You saved me again,' she whispered.

'Not really.' He gave her that lopsided smile of his. 'I think the three men who sat on top of me say otherwise.'

'This is *ridiculous*,' Harold declared. 'You don't even know him and—' His words stopped as Cormac turned his attention to the Grand Duke and held him firmly within his stare. Victoria smirked as her uncle visibly flinched at the action, and two of his security force took a step forward.

Victoria rolled her eyes and tugged Cormac to walk with her.

'I thought you'd be thanking me, Your Royal Highness,' she said without glancing back at her uncle. 'At least this way, you'll be able to marry Alistair off! Sorry, Alistair!'

'I'm going to set Artie on you!' her cousin shouted before the door closed behind them.

CHAPTER FOUR

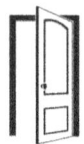

When the two walked back into the Blue Ballroom, everyone's attention turned to them, not that you'd have known it, of course. Her cousins didn't need to actually *look* at her to know what she'd just gone through and how she was feeling, and those familiar with the royal scene carefully masked their curiosity by glancing around the room as they drank and listened to her cousins chatter on about nothing of import.

It was only Cormac's friends that stood openly staring at the pair from their positions tucked in the corner on the far side of the room.

Geri was the first to spot them. She jumped up and down in her pretty little dress and waved her arm over her head, motioning for them to come their way.

Cormac groaned next to her, and Victoria knew he'd spotted the action too.

'She's as subtle as a brick,' he lamented, making Victoria huff a laugh. 'I best go over before she starts bellowing my name across the room or we'll never be invited back. Will you join us?'

She considered it, but she saw Artie look her way and she sighed, knowing if she didn't go and tell him what had transpired behind the closed doors, he'd only turn up at her room later. And if Cormac was going to *kiss* her tonight, she didn't want any interruptions. So, she bit her lip and shook her head, peering up at him with an apology in her eyes.

'I'm sorry, but I know that Artie wants me, and he'll be a nightmare if I don't speak to him first.'

'You don't *have* to speak to him, you know,' Cormac told her. 'If he's such a prick, just ignore him, come with me. I mean, my friends can also be pricks, but they're the nicer kind.'

She chuckled at his words and gently shook her head. 'No, seriously, you don't know Artie.'

'Fair enough.' Cormac shrugged. He made to walk away, but she tightened her fingers still grasped in his hand, making him stop and turn back to her.

'I'll be over as quickly as I can. Order me a gin and tonic, please?' She hadn't drunk anything save for water so far that evening, knowing full well that she'd have to face her grandfather early on. Now the damage was done and as soon as she got Artie off her back, she was *definitely* having a few! 'And food won't be too long either.'

'Finally!' He threw his head back as he spoke, and Victoria shook her head at his dramatics.

'Cormac.' She stopped him just before he made to leave again. He frowned down at her before looking back at Geri who was now using two hands to motion to him. 'Did you mean what you said in there?'

'I said a few words in there, what specifically?' he asked as he made a shooing motion to Geri.

She wanted to ask about the kissing, wanted to know if he was really going to fulfil his promise about what would happen when they did finally kiss. She wanted to grab her necklace again, but the damn thing was tucked away in her jewellery box and she couldn't exactly tug at her mother's diamonds. And she purposefully hadn't worn any rings to ensure she wouldn't fidget nervously. But *how* was she meant to ask here, in a room full of her family and their friends?

Did you really mean you wanted to have sex with me tonight?

Are we going to do it? For real? Where? When? What position should we use?

She told her stupid brain to shut up.

'That I was beautiful?' she blurted out instead and cursed herself. The way he'd looked at her after he'd spoken had told her he thought so even if his own confirmation hadn't been forthcoming.

He frowned down at her, giving her his full attention again. 'I told you I meant that.'

'Yes, you did.' He took her in, his eyes fixed on hers, and she could see that he was trying to work out what was really on her mind. 'Go on,' she said instead of telling him. 'Your friends are waiting for you.'

'That's not what you wanted to ask, is it?' She bit her lip and ducked her head, but a moment later, his finger was under her chin and gently encouraging her to lift her head again and look at him. When she finally met his green gaze, he spoke again. 'Speak to me, Victoria.'

'Did you really mean that you were going to kiss me tonight?' she asked in a rush of breath, making her words almost indistinguishable from one another. Her face flushed hot, and she knew she'd instantly gone bright red. She tried to lower her head again, but he leaned forward, and Victoria's breath caught in her throat as his lips caressed hers in the same teasingly soft kiss they'd offered each other before.

Her heart fluttered and her whole body awakened at the soft touch. She felt herself lean towards him, chasing his lips as he pulled away from her. Her huff of irritation pulled a low chuckle from him.

'Don't scowl at me,' he told her as she glared up at him, her mouth in a very definite pout. He brushed her cheek with the back of his knuckles before his index finger reached out and tapped her protruding lip. 'I told you, when I kiss you properly—which I *will* do later—I'm not going to stop there.'

That love-sick sigh did *not* fall from her lips, she told herself as he smirked at her before walking away with a strong, confident stride. She watched him filter through their guests and stared longer still as he joined his friends. Her pulse fluttered under her skin, wondering just *how* he was going to *kiss* her later.

Would they fall into the bedroom, burning with passion and aching to get each other's clothes off? Maybe he'd throw her up against the door and just kiss her like he was a dying man and she was his last meal. Perhaps he'd hitch her up against the door, wrap her legs around his waist as he impaled her there and then, thrusting into her until she woke everyone up with her screams of pleasure?

Artie's voice drawled in her ear, making her jump. She had no idea how long she stayed there daydreaming about all the ways the two of them could make love that night, and no clue how long she would have remained if she hadn't been disturbed.

'You are such a pain in the royal arse,' he told her. She slowly turned around to the lothario prince and frowned at him.

'And just what have I done to annoy you *this* time?' she asked with a tired sigh.

'I owe Caroline five crowns because of you.'

She rolled her eyes. 'That's really not going to break the bank.'

'I owe Hugh fifty.'

She grimaced at that. That was a bit steeper.

'What was the bet, and *why* does it concern me?' She had no idea why she asked. It was probably something to do with her dress or the fact she still wasn't wearing an engagement ring. Her mind briefly flitted to her jewellery box again and the special ring nestled safely within it. She still hadn't figured out how to approach Cormac with it. He'd probably think it was too gaudy or that perhaps it would enrage her grandfather.

'Because I didn't think you'd actually *love* the bugger.'

All of Victoria's thoughts came to a crashing halt as her cousin's words registered with her brain.

'Pardon?'

'Oh, don't try and feign ignorance, Victoria, it doesn't become you. Your face is far too long to pull it off. Oh!' he added as she stared at him aghast at his comment. 'You can get away with outraged rather well. It helps balance that nose of yours.'

She closed her eyes and slowly began to count to ten, resisting the urge to want to claw her own face off at her cousin's comments—although she'd have to make it to twenty to resist the urge to rip *his* face off.

'Artie,' she managed through clenched teeth. 'Of course, I *love* Cormac. I am *marrying* him.'

'Yeah, and in just a few weeks. Not carrying his spawn already, are you?'

'How- You—' Heat scalded her skin for a completely different reason this time as fury, the kind only Artie could bubble up within someone, overwhelmed her. Her vision began to swim as she overflowed with indignation and white-hot anger at the self-centred, egotistical... *dickhead* that was before her.

'That's enough, Arthur.' Another voice stopped Victoria

from swinging out and hitting him. Her hands stayed clenched at her sides, so hard she was frightened her nails were going to draw blood and leave scars. 'Go and play with the people you *think* are your friends.'

Victoria blinked away the black spots that had filled her vision and saw her Aunt Sophie, the diminutive Grand Duchess, and Alistair's mother, scowling at her nephew.

'I'll have you—'

'Ten people above you, Arthur,' Sophia said with a sniff. 'Go away.' Artie glowered at the future Queen before turning on his heel and storming off. When he didn't glance their way before joining another group, her aunt sighed.

'I think it's about time someone in this family married for love,' Sophie confessed without taking her eyes from Artie. 'Your mother is Richard's only child who actually married someone they fell in love with. It gives me hope the others might. Although, I doubt *he*'—she nodded towards Artie—'will marry for anything other than advantage and prestige.'

Victoria tried to think of something to say, but her tongue didn't seem to want to work. Not that her brain was providing it with anything to respond with. Her Aunt Sophie had always been quiet, had barely ever spoken to her voluntarily and here she was not only talking to her without invite, but speaking out against the way of the family.

'Oh, it's no secret, my dear,' Sophie said as she finally faced Victoria. 'I'd been picked out for Harold years before we finally married, since I was but a child and he already a man, at least in the eyes of the law. It was a match based on paper—titles and gold—not of the heart.' Her eyes glanced towards her husband as he came out of the same door Victoria had stepped through just a few minutes before. A second later, Alistair followed in his wake. 'I had hoped to avoid such a match for Alistair and maybe, with you as an example, it can work that way.'

Victoria tried to process that idea.

She'd always considered Alistair's marriage as already assured, that everyone was just waiting for *her* to go down the aisle first. She really did believe that Alistair would be all but following her down the cathedral's deep blue carpets. But if his mother was against such a match, perhaps her cousin had a chance? Maybe with her in his corner, Alistair would finally be able to stand up to his father who would undoubtedly be the one choosing his son's future bride.

She glanced towards where the Grand Duke and Alistair stood, where it was clear Harold was berating his son again. To give Alistair his due, the prince had his head up, but his eyes didn't meet his father's. Instead, he stared out across the partygoers, focused on the back of the room as he took whatever rebuke his father was throwing at him. Victoria wished he'd stand up to the Duke, to tell him, just once, that he was his own man. It was true that she had failed to do the same—with her father, the King, anyone really—but she wasn't going to wear the crown. How could her cousin one day lead the nation if he was always bowing his head or was unable to meet the eye of his enemy?

'Don't pity him,' Sophie said. 'And don't think him weak. He fights his battles behind closed doors, as a man should. His father could learn a thing or two from my son.' Victoria turned her gaze away from the heirs and back towards her aunt. 'I like you, Victoria, I always have. I might not have always shown it, too aggrieved by your mother's selfishness when she ran off with your father and forced me into a marriage I was far from ready to endure, but I have. I am sorry I allowed your mother's transgressions to cloud my ability to form a friendship with you. I hope going forward that may change?'

Victoria blinked at the Grand Duchess in surprise and bafflement. Had she just called her mother's elopement selfish? That the wonderful love story she'd grown up hearing, wishing for her own version of the fairy tale had been the cause of deep pain for others?

She looked at her aunt properly for the first time and noticed a woman, much younger than Victoria had considered, staring back at her. While she knew there was almost a fourteen-year age difference between the Grand Duke and Duchess, she'd never really seen it before. Sophie always stood so stoically at her husband's side, a prim and proper consort for the future king. She dressed like she was approaching seventy rather than the fifty-four years she was. It was the complete opposite to her own parents, who had just over fifteen years difference. Her father had always seemed younger, almost as youthful as his young wife.

The Duchess and Princess Melinda had been the same age, yet Victoria could never imagine her mother looking as old or dowdy as the woman before her. She glanced towards where her Aunt Amelia stood, two years older than Sophie, yet looking twenty her junior. She often got comments describing her more akin to one of the King's granddaughters than his actual daughter. Would her mother have looked more like Amelia?

It was a cruel game to play, and not one Victoria wanted to indulge.

And that was when the future queen's words hit home. She was the same age as her mother would be, meaning they were the same age when they got married, just a day apart. Had Sophie been promised more time before she was supposed to wed Harold and her mother's elopement had ruined that? In that sense, her mother's actions could very well be construed as selfish and, in her aunt's eyes, unforgivable.

'That would be nice, Auntie,' Victoria said, finally finding her tongue untied. Sophie nodded her approval and glanced towards where her husband and son were. The Grand Duke pointed his finger at Alistair, saying one last thing before he turned on his heel and stormed away into the crowd.

'He trusts you,' Sophie said as she watched her son gather himself together. He took a deep breath before putting on a smile and glancing around the room. His eyes landed on Victoria and his mother and he headed towards them. 'Please guide him well when he comes to you.'

'Mother, Victoria, interesting to see you two chatting. Might I enquire the occasion?'

'Don't be a brat,' Sophie said with a put-upon sigh. 'I'm not your enemy and neither is Victoria.' And before Victoria could say anything, the Grand Duchess turned and left the two of them. Victoria watched her go, completely baffled as to what on earth had just happened.

'What were you two talking about?' Alistair asked, unable to keep the curiosity from his voice. It took Victoria a moment to try and piece together what exactly she *could* say they'd been discussing.

'Love,' she finally settled on. The prince snorted.

'Like she knows what that is.'

'Don't be a dick,' Victoria frowned as she looked at Alistair. She weighed up if she should say anything more to the Prince when he snagged a waiter and ordered a double scotch. She raised her brows at such a drink.

'Don't,' was all he said. She held up her hands in mock surrender.

'Come on'—she slipped her arm through his—'let's go and see how *normal* people act at parties,' she said with a sigh as she led him to Cormac and his friends, putting her conversation with her aunt out of her head.

As they were halfway across the room, Cormac turned

TAKING HIM

and spotted the royal cousins heading towards them. He smiled at her, a wide beaming smile that reached his eyes and made them seem to glow in the warm light of the room. Victoria's heart began to race, and she had to swallow the sudden moisture that gathered in her mouth at the sight of her future husband... Who was going to *kiss* her tonight. Her knees felt weak at the thought, and she was glad Alistair was at her side to lead her the rest of the way.

'You okay?' Alistair asked quietly as she stumbled ever so slightly.

'That's the man I'm going to marry,' her mouth said instead of the *yes, I'm fine* her brain wanted to spit at him. Alistair's warm chuckle at her side only made her brain curse him and her body even more.

'I really am happy for you,' Alistair told her. 'I'm glad that one of us gets to have our heart lead us down the aisle.'

She blinked at the words. Were she and Cormac *that good* at acting that they were able to convince even her family that they were in love?

Her brain went eerily quiet at that question, her heart thundering in her chest as they got closer to the group. She licked her lips, suddenly nervous, as Cormac took a step towards them.

'I'll take it from here,' he said to Alistair and held out his arm to her. She looked up at him and felt her world tilt. What the hell was wrong with her?

'You're going to kiss me tonight.' Her mouth once again spoke without her brain telling it to. The beaming smile he'd been giving her turned into a salacious grin, and she felt her breath hitch as he leaned down toward her. But instead of aiming for her mouth, he instead kissed her cheek.

'How about we bail out early and go and do some kissing now?' His breath was warm against her skin as he murmured his words in her ear, before pressing another kiss just below it. She gasped and turned to him, her nose nudging against his cheek as her body tingled in anticipation of his touch. She wanted to trace his strong jaw with her lips, kiss her way down his neck as she undid that bow tie that made him look so damn sexy, and slowly undo his buttons one by one as she followed them downwards with her mouth.

'What do you say, princess?' he murmured as his hands settled on her waist and pulled her closer to him. Was he going to kiss her right here? Would he throw her over his shoulder and march them off to their room that instant if she just said yes? God, she hoped so!

'*Yes.*' She breathed the word and he groaned in pleasure and need.

'Quickest way out?' he asked as he pressed another kiss to her neck. 'Which door?'

'The one we—'

A ringing of a bell trilled across the room, jarring Victoria and Cormac from their private bubble.

'Dinner is served!' the Master of Ceremonies called out and a murmur of pleasure filled the room.

'Later, princess,' Cormac said, taking a step back from her. He took her hand, as she stared at him with such disappointment, and lifted it to his lips to press a kiss to it. 'I promise. Every wish, every desire you have, I will fulfil.'

She whimpered in frustration as they began to walk towards the state room where their fancy dinner would be served. She didn't want dinner; she wanted the man next to her!

'Fifty crowns!' she heard Hugh's voice shout in elation across the room. 'Pay up, Artie!'

Victoria groaned.

TAKING HIM

SINCE HE'D GOT ENGAGED—AND THAT WAS STILL WEIRD TO think about—Cormac felt that he'd spent more time standing in front of doors building up the courage to go through them than at any other point in his life. And that was saying something, considering that at sixteen, he'd thought waiting to go into the Headmaster's office after being caught locked in Jessica's embrace, sucking a hickey onto her neck with his hand up her skirt was always going to be where he'd needed the most courage.

Then when he was eighteen, he'd figured that was wrong and there was no way he'd ever need as much strength as he did standing at the hospital doors waiting to go and collect his brother, alone, as his new guardian.

At twenty, he'd actually figured raising a baby was easy compared to standing in front of the court doors as they finally repossessed the house his parents had left him; he'd failed to make the mortgage payments for more than six months after being scammed out of the lump sum he'd received in their will.

And at twenty-three, there had been the doors to the first strip club he'd worked at as a *hot butler*, serving drinks in just a G-string, and stupid shirt collar, tie, and cuffs.

But now, at twenty-five, he found himself constantly pausing in front of any bedroom door that Victoria stood behind, reminding himself not to give in to temptation, to keep his hands to himself, to make their first time the right time... once he was able to get over the whole inequality between them thing. And tonight was that night. He'd seen it when she stood in front of the King, when she'd attacked a Guard to get to him, when she'd demanded things and been denied them, just as he had been throughout his life.

She might be a lady of the realm, but just like everyone else, there were people she had to bow to, had to submit to. She might have money and a title, but she wasn't too far different from him in the grand scheme of things—they both had to prostrate themselves at the feet of others.

He took a breath and scratched at his ear as he stood staring at the ornate door into their bedroom somewhere deep in the palace. He'd tucked a very tired James into bed and had no other reason to delay walking into their room and doing what he'd promised.

But that was the thing; he'd promised it in the heat of the moment, and now the moment was gone, he wasn't quite sure how to approach his betrothed. Save for Jessica, all his moments of passion had been quick fumbles in the back of cars, in club or pub toilets, or down dark alleyways.

He wasn't proud of his experiences, but he'd needed the occasional touch of a woman to remind himself that he was still a man, a desirable one, rather than just a loser as he'd often felt. Afterwards when the moment of sexual euphoria had subsided, he'd only felt a bigger loser. He didn't want to feel that way with Victoria.

But, he thought with a sigh, Victoria was beautiful, elegant, classy, *and* sexy. She wouldn't have lowered herself to such a fumble, she was *lady* after all. He scoffed at the idea of taking her down a dark alleyway or following her into the back seat of a car to do more than drive somewhere—although there had been that moment in the back of the Rolls when they'd returned from the solicitors. Maybe Victoria wouldn't be averse to driving out somewhere nice and quiet and steaming up some windows...

They should have just left the party as soon as he'd said the words, found a room somewhere and locked themselves inside for a while. Instead, he'd had to watch her across that ridiculously long table, around huge candelabras, and between waiters' arms as they poured drink after drink to everyone. There'd been toasts to their hosts and then dancing—not that he'd spent much time with Victoria in his arms then either, as she'd been whisked off by almost every man in the room. He'd even seen her taking a turn with a surprisingly graceful Axel!

'You know if you stand there any longer, the maids will start to dust you.' Cormac jumped as Victoria's voice called from the other side of the door. He looked around to see how she knew it was him when she tapped the wood. 'Peephole.'

He sighed when he saw the tiny glass spyhole hidden deep in the door's intricate carvings and opened it, stepping inside quickly, and closing it behind him. The room was bathed in just the glow from the fire that shimmered gently in its place; it invited you to snuggle up on the giant, luxurious bed that dominated the room and just drift off to sleep wrapped in warmth and its soft hues.

That was if a goddess wasn't standing at its foot.

Victoria still wore her stiletto shoes, and her long legs were clad in her sheer black stockings. The lace of her stocking tops was just visible under the silky robe tied loosely at her waist, giving him a glimpse of what she had on underneath, which wasn't a lot—a tiny pair of lacy panties and a matching bra.

Whatever plan he might have formed, would have been wasted as every thought left his head as she sunk her teeth into her plump lower lip, staring up at him through her long, dark lashes, and swayed slightly on the spot, giving him tantalising glimpses of her bare stomach before the robe hid it again.

Victoria was certainly *not* like women he'd had before. He didn't just want to spend himself and push her away. No, he wanted to fall at her feet and worship her. To murmur prayers of devotion into her skin as his lips pressed their blessings upon her. He wanted to take his time with her, to love her and cherish her and make her feel as no other man had. He wanted to do so much and yet his feet weren't moving towards her, his mouth was simply opening and closing as it tried to say something—*anything*—but his brain could do nothing but tell him to keep his focus on the woman before him.

'You look tired,' she said, giving him an exaggerated pout.

'I'm not—I mean, I am, but I'm not.' He had no idea what he was saying as he stepped towards her, his hands reaching out to touch that satiny robe, to get his fingers underneath it and pull it away. She shouldn't be wearing anything, he decided.

She sucked her lower lip back between her teeth and Cormac wanted to tell her to stop, that if anyone was going to nibble that lip, it would be him. But he decided as he stopped before her, actions spoke louder than words.

He reached up, his strong fingers gently taking her chin, and his thumb slowly pulled her lip free.

'I'm going to kiss you now.' His voice was deep, far deeper than he'd ever heard it, and he resisted the urge to clear his throat as he bent his head to finally claim his prize.

He heard her little gasp a second before their lips met. He teased her, giving her that same gentle caress they'd shared a few times before, causing her to whimper in disappointment. He resisted the urge to smile as much as he defied his desire to gather her to him. He wanted to take his time, to go slow and—

Umph!

His breath was knocked from him as Victoria grabbed the lapels of his jacket and pulled him to her, pressing their bodies together and capturing his lips for the first time properly.

The idea of going slow immediately disappeared from his mind as he gathered her up in his arms, holding her tight as she opened to him and allowed him to deepen the kiss.

Her hands slid into his jacket and began to push it off his shoulders and he quickly helped, shrugging out of it as quickly as he could.

They stood entwined for what felt like an eternity, when it was but a few seconds before they finally had to part to catch their breaths.

'I thought you'd never kiss me,' Victoria panted as she leaned back to gaze up at him, her eyes filled with desire.

'I told you I was gonna.'

She made a *hmm* noise, tilting her head and considering him, her perfect teeth sinking back into the plumpness of her mouth. He wanted to suckle it again, but her hands slipping up his shoulders to pull at his bow tie hindered him from doing just that.

'You don't need this,' she told him as she made deft work of undoing her earlier handiwork and pulling the strip of expensive fabric from his collar. She made to throw it to one side, but paused as she looked at the bow tie, considering it for a second before glancing back at him with a naughty glint in her eye. 'At least not tonight. We'll save that for another time.'

Cormac felt his already interested cock get a whole lot more attentive at her suggestion.

'I thought you were a *lady*,' he said as she threw the tie away.

'Out there,' she said, nodding towards the door as she began to work on undoing the buttons on his shirt. 'Not in the bedroom.'

He groaned at her words as he realised that he had completely misjudged the woman in his arms and hurriedly helped her with the task at hand. As soon as his shirt was off, her lips were on his again, her hands around his neck, fingers sliding into his blond locks so she could return his kiss just as ferociously.

When his hands moved to undo her belt, she broke the kiss, trailing her lips down his neck to his chest as she slapped his wandering digits away. She kissed her way along his collar bone and slowly down his chest. The jangle of his belt only intensified his cock's response and if she wasn't careful, she was going to get a sneak peek of what he had to offer before she fully unwrapped him.

He gasped as her finger, running up the zip of his trousers, lightly traced his now straining length. He bit back the groan, trying to remain in control, but as she met his eyes and that salacious smirk returned, he knew there was no denying which of them was running the show. He had definitely misjudged her.

She kept her eyes on his as she unbuttoned his trousers before slowly pulling down his zip, inch by torturous inch. She gaze lingered as she leaned forward and pressed a kiss to his stomach, while pushing his trousers all the way down to his ankles. She ran her hands up his thighs, sliding her delicate fingers towards his boxer shorts all while still staring up at him. He was hypnotised, bewitched, totally at her mercy, and unable to look away as her fingers crept over his boxers, walking their way up either side of his now very alert cock before slipping inside the elastic band and gently pulling them away from his skin.

He swallowed as she eased them over his throbbing erection and pushed them down to his knees where they fell to the floor to join his trousers, before she leaned forward, still keeping her gaze fixed on him, and flicked her warm, wet tongue out to trace the length of his shaft.

He sucked his breath in between his teeth and canted his head back, eyes tightly closed as she sat up on her knees and with excruciating slowness slid her lips over the head of his erection. His fingers flexed into fists at his side, so he didn't twist them into her hair and hold her head as he thrust into her mouth. He allowed her to set the pace, to explore him as she wanted, to taste him at her leisure... even if it killed him.

He groaned as she swirled her tongue, and he couldn't help the push of his hips forward ever so slightly. Her hands slid around his waist and held his body still as she worked him slowly and carefully towards the brink of ecstasy.

It had been too long since he'd had a partner, too long since he'd even kissed anyone, that to have the feel of a woman pleasing him with her mouth, enveloping him in wet heat was just too much. His hand had done a fine job up to today, but he silently apologised to it as he relegated it back to the land of *never again*, knowing he and Victoria could happily explore one another for the rest of their lives.

'Princess, stop,' he whispered as she bobbed at an excruciatingly slow pace. 'I want to- I need to—'

She slowly drew her lips up his length and pulled away, dropping a kiss to his glistening head as she sat back and looked up him.

'What, Cormac? What do you want?'

'You,' he said, his voice deep and gravelly. 'I want you.'

A smile curved her lips and Victoria pushed herself to her feet. She bit her lip, looking up at him coyly as she took a step back and languidly began to untie the belt of her robe.

When the knot was undone, she let the sash drop to the sides, but made no move to slip the silky fabric from her shoulders. Cormac groaned as she turned and took a few more steps out of his reach.

He wanted to follow her, to grab her and turn her to him, to divest her of the damn robe before he showed her that he wasn't a loser anymore, that he could be her equal. But she stopped before he could act, glancing at him over her shoulder, ensuring he was watching before she slowly pushed the robe, letting it fall from her body to reveal herself to him.

He felt the breath knocked from him as his eyes travelled

down her body, over her peachy skin until he saw that her panties hid nothing of her pert little rear.

'Victoria, please,' he pleaded when she moved towards him again. She reached up, sliding her hands over his shoulders.

'Cormac,' she whispered, her lips brushing his. Her eyelashes fluttered closed as she breathed in his scent and pushed herself against him, trapping his cock between them. 'I've wanted you from our first meeting,' she confessed, and Cormac internally cheered that it hadn't just been one-sided.

'I know this isn't the perfect set up for us,' she continued breathily. 'But I think we can make it work; I think we could have something *special* if we try.'

'Oh, you're special, princess,' he told her before he finally took her lips with his. Everything within him roared in jubilation as she gasped at the contact before melting into his body. His arms wrapped around her, holding her close. He moved them, slowly, until Victoria's knees hit the back of the bed and Cormac gently lowered her to the mattress, nestling himself between her legs.

He threw his head back, squeezing his eyes closed as he gathered his self-control together as Victoria once more tried to take the lead; moving her hips, grinding against his begging cock, trying to entice him to sheath himself deep within her. The lacy fabric of her panties covered her so little it was barely a barrier between them. It would be so easy to nudge it to one side and give her exactly what she was asking for.

'Not yet,' he groaned between his teeth as his hips met her thrusts on their own accord, and he begged his body to calm down, to hold back just a few minutes.

'Please,' she whispered as she leaned up and kissed his neck, trailing her lips down to his shoulders, as she wrapped her legs around his hips. 'I want this... you... so much.'

He buried his head in the crook of her shoulder. He wanted to spend more time worshipping her; it had been so long since he'd had the chance to worship any woman the way they deserved, but it was because of exactly that reason he knew if he didn't do it now, it would be a very short devotional indeed.

Pulling away, he gently took her arms in his hands and pushed them into the bed. She wiggled against him, pouting and huffing as she tried to touch him once more.

'Just this.' He pressed his lips to the skin above the small cup of her bra. 'Just let me do this.' He felt her arms go slack as he pressed another kiss between her breasts. Kissing his way down her body, over her trembling stomach, he reached the line of her naughty underwear and finally released her hands to carefully take the delicate lace and slide it over her hips and down her legs.

He pressed kisses to her hip and at the juncture of her thigh and her enticing sex as he inched her panties lower. She mewed as he moved down her thigh with his mouth and he couldn't help the small smirk forming, knowing exactly where she'd hoped his lips would go.

With her panties removed, he made his way back up her body until he once more was nestled against her, and she was able to slide one of her legs over his hip.

'Are you sure this is okay?' he whispered into her skin as he nipped kisses along her throat. 'I could do so much—'

'No! I mean yes! Oh, God, yes!' she panted as she wiggled her body beneath him. 'This, right now. I want you, Cormac.'

He wrapped his arm around her, holding her close as he adjusted his hips. His hand slipped between them, his finger softly pressing through the small curl of hair she had.

'Cormac!' she cried, arching her back as he found her small nub and gently massaged it. 'Oh!' Her hips bucked up and Cormac sheathed himself in her, groaning in pleasure as she tightened around him and pulled him deeper by wrapping her legs around him.

'Fuck, Victoria,' he breathed as finally moved within her. His hips thrusting gently, his finger trying to match his movements, to help her get there as fast as he was going to.

She trembled, meeting his movements with her own as he built their rhythm and encouraged her to take her pleasure. The soft gasps and little noises that fell from her lips told him she was close, and he pushed faster, the heels of her shoes against his bare arse a pleasurable little pain to remind him of the magnificent goddess that she was.

'Cormac?' She said the name in almost a question, and he pulled away from the hollow of her neck and met her eyes. They were half closed in sweet pleasure, but what he could see was almost golden in colour from the light of the fire. He was mesmerised, trapped in their glow as his name fell over her lips again and again.

Her hand reached up to cup his cheek, and she pulled him to her, capturing his bottom lip between hers and gently pulling it, encouraging him to take what she offered.

He kissed her like he was a starving man being offered a feast, frightened his servers would suddenly change their minds and take it all away. His tongue met hers, caressing it as she bucked against him when she reached her peak, her cries becoming louder as she stood at the precipice and prepared to fall.

'Victoria, my princess,' he whispered against her lips. 'Be mine.'

And she was.

Her body tightened around him, her back arched and she canted her head back. Her lips parted as she silently cried out in pleasure. He paused to watch her, marvelling at her beauty. This was the woman he was about to marry, the woman who hoped to carry and bear his child. He was going to be entangled with this woman for the rest of his life and he felt like the luckiest man alive.

All the other men had been idiots, not recognising her beauty or her heart, thinking her merely a title, an access to higher things. If she told him tomorrow there was no money coming from the will and that her grandfather had stripped all support from her too, he wouldn't care. They'd face the world together and come out on top.

He kissed her lips, her chin, down her neck again as he began to move once more, chasing his own completion. Something deep inside him whispered only she could give that to him, but he ignored it as he raced to the end, unwilling to entertain such thoughts.

When he cried out, it was her name that fell from his lips, chanting it as if it was an incantation, but for what, he had no idea.

'I really like kissing,' Victoria said a little breathlessly as she lay beside him a few minutes later. 'I think we should kiss again.'

He smiled at the ceiling as he heard her roll over to face him. 'I might be twenty-five, but I do need a little bit of recovery time.'

'Really?' she asked, and he felt his body jump as her fingers gently traced up his softening cock. It twitched in interest, but he knew it was in vain.

'He'll need fifteen minutes,' he said as he turned to meet her pouting face. 'But I supposed I could kiss you somewhere other than this delectable mouth.' He tapped her lips with this finger as he shifted over to meet her. The pout turned into a slow smile as she lay back against the bed covers and welcomed his kisses.

∼

'CORMAC,' VICTORIA SAID. HER VOICE WAS QUIET, AND WHEN he peeled one eye open, he knew it was still the dead of night. The fire's flame had turned the wood to red embers, casting their room deep in the palace into shadows, the light of the cinders only just reaching the bed. 'Cormac, are you awake?'

'I am now,' he groaned, turning onto his back. He expected Victoria to be lying there, staring up at the ceiling, unable to sleep despite all the physical exercise they'd shared that night. If she wanted it again...

But no, Victoria knelt on the bed, hidden almost all in shadow, her long hair loose and hanging around her shoulders, hiding some of her face. In her hands lay an open ring box and Cormac felt his chest tighten, his breath stop, and his heart speed up at the sight of the large, blue stone of the ring.

Holy shit! That was one hell of an engagement ring.

'It's *La Larme Bleue*, it means—'

'*The Blue Tear*,' he said automatically. He might not follow the gossip pages like Geri did, but even he knew the stories surrounding one of the most famous jewels in Avalonian history.

'It was my mother's,' she said. Finally, Cormac looked up, noticing for the first time that she wasn't looking at him. Instead, her gaze was fixed upon the ring in the box, a sad smile playing at her lips. 'It was the only thing my great-grandmother bequeathed to her on her death bed. My grandfather was livid.' She smirked at that comment and Cormac couldn't help the smile tugging at the corners of his mouth after meeting the man earlier that evening.

She turned the ring slightly, and the light caught it just right for him to see the magic within. The tiny flaws in the stone—the reason why the jeweller, Tavernier, had cut it away from *Le bleu de France*, later the *Hope Diamond*—made the large offcut look as if it had a swirl of stars, a whole galaxy, trapped within its blue depths. Ironic that they were the very reason it was now counted as one of the most beautiful of all jewels in the world.

'I know,' Victoria said with a grin as she finally turned her attention to him and caught his awed expression. 'I believe I had the same look when I first saw it.'

'You want to use this as our engagement ring?' he asked, sitting up properly. He brushed a strand of her long hair behind her ear and tilted her face so he could see her properly in the dim light. He'd been wondering what to do about the ring, if he should go and buy one, if she had one lined up already—as she had with most of the wedding things—but this seemed... perfect. Especially if it would annoy the King!

'Yes,' she said. 'My mother always told me that one day, when I found the man of my dreams, I'd wear this ring to show the world that he was accepted by her and my father, no matter who he was.'

'Unlike *your* father?'

She bobbed her head in agreement. 'Unofficially, they disowned her. Gave her Renfrew Hall and told her to never visit them again beyond her official capacity. She never did. Anytime they met with her, they did so only in the company of others; royal events, family occasions that had some sort of public window—photographers, reporters, etcetera.

'My grandparents, and aunts and uncles, didn't meet me until my baptism,' she confessed. 'Even though they told the public I was a precious addition to their family—their first grandchild after all. Of course, over the years, with the invention of the internet, and social media, there are plenty of rumours floating around about there being a rift in the family despite Grandfather's best intentions to keep it quiet. And to be fair, while I don't get along with my cousins—or at least most of them—the animosity their parents and the King hold isn't there. It's more a snooty thing than anything else. We're the lowest of the low and everyone wants to be as high as they can in our family. The higher you are, the closer to the Crown you are, and thus the power.'

Cormac blinked as he tried to process what she was really telling him. Geri had made sure he was *well* informed of the theories that whipped around the internet—that Princess Melinda had been disavowed, that she wasn't really the King's daughter, that Patrick Snape had bought her, or stolen her... Geri had never believed any of them, of course, and told him he shouldn't either. However, the Avalonian Royal Family was the closest, most tight-knit family of any of the monarchies left in the modern world. Now, he wondered what other worms the can held.

'Any skeletons in your closet?' she asked with an empty laugh.

Conner O'Malley's face flashed in his head briefly, but he quickly closed the door on that thought and shook his head *no*.

'I think your contacts found them all,' he said, referring to the file she'd had compiled on him. He hated how he was able to lie so well to her.

'The King has no control over me,' she suddenly blurted out. 'He can't say who I marry, unlike some of my cousins. My title is only one of courtesy so he has no right to deny me my choice in husband—which is why he didn't try and forbid it this evening—but he will try and poke his nose in. He'll try and get involved. He might even try and get you to walk away from this'—she waved her finger back and forth between them—'so I want to ensure you have your eyes wide open if—'

'Victoria.' He said her name firmly, stopping her rambling, and put his hands over hers, gently removing the box from her grasp. He took the ring from its velvety bed and held it out to her. 'I might not be the man of your dreams, but I'll not stand in your way of achieving them. Will you do me the honour of becoming my wife?'

'Yes,' she said, her mouth breaking into a wide smile as he slipped the ring onto her finger. She admired it for a moment, before rising to her knees and throwing her arms around him, her bare breasts pushing against his chest as she captured his lips in an impassioned kiss.

As they sank back into the pillows, her body covering his, Cormac decided that he really wasn't getting a bad deal out of this after all.

CHAPTER FIVE

'Relax,' Victoria said taking his hand in hers to stop him fidgeting. The soft pad of her thumb gently caressed his palm, and he instantly felt himself doing exactly as she said.

'I think I'd feel better if we could just go *in* there,' he muttered and Victoria *tsked* and shook her head. They'd already been over this half a dozen times, he knew, but it was so strange to wait on someone coming into *your* home to be settled by someone else, before the two of them were allowed to be *presented*. It was an idea he wanted to scoff at, but Victoria assured him that once they were married and she relinquished her title as *The Lady Snape*, they'd be able to sit around in their underwear all day if he so wished.

His lip curled up slightly, both amused and incredibly turned on at the idea of *Victoria* being sprawled across one of the couches in just her bra, tiny knickers, and stockings. Damn, he *loved* those stockings.

'Do you think she'll believe us?' he whispered. She smiled up at him, that tiny soft smile that turned her eyes warm and gentle. Every time she offered him that smile, he felt a little bit of his heart melt.

'I do.'

'Not for four more weeks,' he chuckled as he reached down to cup her cheek before brushing her lips with his.

He couldn't help it. Since their engagement party, it was difficult to keep his hands off her. He had to be careful kissing her around James because one turned into two, and two turned into a very heavy make-out session and his little brother had walked in on them just two days ago. They'd been watching TV in the sitting room when they'd started, and things had quickly turned heated. Victoria had been straddling his lap, topless, her head thrown back as he lavished her breasts with attention when they'd heard James' footsteps on the stairs.

There had been a mad scramble to figure out where they'd thrown her blouse and Victoria had ended up running from the room before James had stumbled in, rubbing his eyes from his afternoon nap.

Since then, they'd been very careful. Victoria was adamant she didn't want to run into Merryweather in the hallways semi-naked again—he wished he'd seen *that*.

Cormac had to admit, when left to their own devices, life was actually coming along nicely. He and Victoria were talking much more freely, feeling the ability to share more about themselves. There were times when Victoria would be talking away about something, and he'd find himself just staring at her, smiling, and if life were different, if they'd met in some other way—if she hadn't had to buy him or he hadn't been poor—the two of them could have had something real.

Once or twice, he'd wondered if they still could?

His lessons in *gentleman-like behaviour* were progressing. Merryweather managed to find time to teach him about the way rich people ate, when you used the funny looking knives and forks, why there were three different glasses on the table, and how to eat a snail—which James had found hilarious until it came his turn to try! The butler had even taken to teaching him about wine. Who knew there was more to it than just red and white? Apparently, everyone but him, Geri had replied to the message he'd sent her after his first tasting.

But he'd still been damn proud of himself last night for recalling everything Merryweather had told him last week. He'd even been able to tell a Sauvignon Blanc from a Pinot Grigio! That might have been because he remembered the sauvignon smelling more—*a stronger aroma, sir*—but he took that as a win.

And he had to admit, he'd enjoyed spoiling James to new clothes, watching him running around a store and picking out things *he* liked. He'd been surprised to find that James had far more sophisticated tastes than he'd ever imagined! Cormac had always picked out jeans and trainers for him but given the choice, James went for the cutest chinos and "grown-up shoes" as he'd called them, preferring jumpers and polo shirts to t-shirts with superheroes on them.

Cormac would never tell another living soul, but he'd discovered he liked shopping for himself too. It was much more fun searching for clothes when you had the money to do so. And who knew he'd look so damn good in a shirt and blazer?

Everyone, according to Victoria.

He made to deepen the kiss when there was a tap at the door of where they were waiting.

'Excuse me, ma'am, sir,' Merryweather said as he opened the door. 'But Ms Adams is waiting.'

'Of course, Merryweather, thank you,' Victoria said, but her eyes were gazing up longingly at Cormac and he knew that tonight would be another spectacular night in their bed. He couldn't wait.

The older man nodded before turning and leaving the two of them to fix themselves.

'Ready?' she asked.

'Lead the way!' He motioned for her to go first and followed in her wake.

When they entered the room, the woman, Ms Adams, stood and dipped her head to both.

'My lady,' the tall blonde woman said with a voice so soft, Cormac almost didn't hear her. He wondered how the hell she was a journalist if she spoke so quietly. Didn't they all yell at people to get their attention and be *the one* to ask a question?

'Thank you for joining us, Ms Adams, and please, take a seat.' Victoria gestured to the chair the woman had risen from as she took her own seat on the couch where Cormac would sit next to her, holding her hand throughout the interview. The whole meeting had been entirely scripted by Victoria's secretary, Kirstie, and not just the questions they'd be asked and the replies they'd give. Oh no, she'd told them what to wear, where to sit—and *how*—and the exact time it would take.

'Please, call me Maxine, and I *love* your dress,' the reporter said to Victoria, who acted a little coyly.

'Thank you,' she said, dipping her head. 'Cormac bought it for me.' Her fingers entwined with his on his knee and he brought her hand further into his lap to be embraced in both his hands as he smiled back at her. He should have been an actor instead of a stripper, he decided. He'd have made a *fortune*!

You already have, his mind taunted him.

'Now, I'm sure you're busy,' the reporter began. 'So how about we get straight to it?' She took out a notebook and pen and Cormac raised his brows in surprise. He imagined a recording device; a dictation machine or phone app, something that would ensure that a single word didn't get missed.

'We don't use recording devices for royal interviews; even press conferences at the palace are pen and paper only,' Maxine told him, seeing his surprise. 'Order of his Majesty, the King.' Cormac ensured he kept his face neutral at the mention of King Richard.

'So,' Maxine began again. 'A very whirlwind romance; how did you meet? *When* did you meet? Lady Snape, you were dating very recently, how does that fit into the story?'

Victoria chuckled softly and dipped her head in a show of bashfulness. 'It gets us to our engagement,' she admitted. 'But we met well before that. Cormac and I had met one afternoon while I was shopping. I dropped a bottle of water and he stopped it from rolling away.' A stupidly simple meet-cute, Kirstie had described it. Could have happened to anyone and so the public would love it.

'I picked it up and handed it to her and got caught in those beautiful golden eyes,' Cormac finished.

'I have to say, I saw him and forgot my words. I don't think I ever thanked him for fetching it for me.'

'Nope, still waiting,' Cormac said with an exaggerated slow shake of his head. 'But she took the bottle, and I asked if maybe she fancied getting a coffee instead.'

'How forward!' the reporter said, scribbling something down on her paper.

'I thought so,' Victoria laughed. 'But apparently it's what *everyone* does! Probably explains why I was single for so long!'

'I, for one, am glad of that!' Cormac brought her hand up to his lips and pressed a kiss to it as he stared at Victoria. She gave him that heart-softening smile again and he found his lips lingering, as he fought off the urge to kiss her properly. He cleared his throat as he looked away and noticed that the reporter had been following their every move.

'So, was it love at first sight?' Maxine asked, glancing at her pad. Both Victoria and Cormac shook their heads.

'Definitely instant attraction though,' Victoria said, and Cormac enthusiastically nodded in agreement.

'She wouldn't give me her number,' he laughed. 'Said it wasn't protocol or something, but promised she'd be in touch.'

'Ah, so that's how it started?'

Victoria bit her lip and peered coyly at Cormac from the corner of her eye.

'I may *not* have called him. I chickened out; what if he didn't answer? What if he said *no*? So, I…' She trailed off and looked up at her betrothed who feigned exasperation with a roll of his eyes.

'She "accidentally"'—he dropped her hand for a moment to do the air quotes—'bumped into me again a fortnight later. Said she'd lost my number and immediately invited me out to lunch. After that, she gave me *her* number.'

'And he called that evening, thanked me for lunch, and we ended up chatting for what felt like hours.'

'It was,' he confirmed. 'I ran out of minutes—which she didn't understand.'

'Yes,' Victoria said with a slow nod. 'We got on so well, we were deeply attracted to one another, but we were from vastly different worlds. It was… *difficult.*'

Cormac snorted a laugh at her words. 'Difficult is an understatement. Victoria was frightened of being seen with me in case her father didn't approve, or King Richard thought me beneath her. I didn't want the palaver that came with her lifestyle, the constant media attention and being paraded in front of the public. And I certainly didn't want James being dragged through it.'

He gritted his teeth together for the next bit. He hated—absolutely *hated*—the idea of James being shown to the world, but Victoria had advised him a glimpse of his brother would satisfy their curiosity and stop them clamouring for something—*anything*—on him. In the long run, it would give them fewer problems. He bit back the sigh as Maxine's eyes lit up.

'He's your son, yes?'

That made Cormac blink. He'd never, ever referred to James as his son.

'No,' he said, his voice turning quite serious. 'James is my brother. I became his legal guardian when our parents died not long after he was born.'

'Oh.' The reporter quickly scribbled something down. 'I see, and is he... Does he know this or does he refer to you as Dad?'

'What? No!'

Victoria's fingers tightened on his minutely; he had to be cool, he had to be calm. *Keep your tone light and conversational,* had been her earlier instructions.

'James is aware that I'm his brother. I wouldn't lie to him about where he came from. Our parents loved both of us too much to deny them the acknowledgement of who they are to James.'

Maxine looked down at her notes again, her brow lined with confusion. 'But isn't he only six?'

Cormac opened his mouth to reply, but Victoria jumped in. 'Yes, and so *very* clever. He's so far ahead of his peers that his teachers are struggling to keep him engaged. It's why he'll be going to Highbourne Academy next year.'

'Oh, your old school!' The reporter made another scribble.

'Yes,' Victoria agreed. 'But he'll be joining the likes of my sisters as an alumnus of their accelerated programme over their regular curricula.'

'I see'—another note—'fascinating.' Cormac didn't think she thought it so and wondered if Victoria had been right all along. Perhaps it had been the speculation of him having a child that had caught the attention of the media, that maybe there was an ex-girlfriend out there, waiting in the wings to spring out at the wedding and object, or maybe file for rights over James or something equally soap opera dramatic.

'So, if you two started dating before the death of your father,' Maxine moved back to the real reason she was here. 'Why the very public dates after you exited your mourning period?'

'Well,' Victoria began with a deep breath. 'Cormac and I disagreed on certain things.'

Cormac snorted. 'Understatement.'

'I decided that I was approaching my mid-thirties, if I loved someone, I should be with them and not worrying what my father or my grandfather thought. I was also fed up of hiding away; never going anywhere or never being able to go out with Cormac and his friends because he didn't think the public would understand. Cormac thought they'd see him as a plaything for me because of his age, or as a gold digger, when really that's so far from the truth.'

'I also wanted to protect James from media scrutiny, and we hope that the press and the public respect that wish,' he added. Maxine nodded her head in a sympathetic way.

'We broke up shortly before my father died and I didn't cope very well.' Victoria lowered her voice as she spoke, making the other woman lean forward to hear her words. 'When Cormac heard the news of my father's passing, he called and checked up on me; we spoke for a bit and I so longed to be with him again. I wanted to reconcile, but he still couldn't cope with the idea of the publicity.'

'I thought it would eventually cause a rift between us,' Cormac added. 'And that we'd end up hating one another, when at least we had parted as friends.'

'And I felt so worthless,' Victoria admitted, shrinking in on herself. Cormac dropped her hand and wrapped his arm around her, pulling her close and pressing a kiss to her head as he heard the woman across from him quickly writing her notes. 'I rushed the mourning period for Daddy just to get back at you,' she whispered.

Cormac felt his heart ache at her forlorn *confession*. It was partly true; she'd told him when they'd been discussing what to say; she'd rushed it so she could find a husband. He just happened to be the one she'd found.

'But it worked out in the end,' he reminded her, talking quietly into her ear, but loud enough for the woman across from them to overhear. 'You got me and I'm sure that your father would be incredibly happy that *you're* finally happy.'

He felt her head nod against his chest.

'As you can see,' Cormac said, raising his head just enough to look at the reporter. 'Things are still a little tender for her.'

The woman tried to disguise glee at their little moment with a frown to make her more sombre, but the constant twitching of her mouth gave her away. 'I understand.'

'Victoria threw herself into dating and made sure it was all over the media, knowing it would drive me mad. Finally, when one date went a little wrong, and she sought shelter at a club before a Guard could come and take her to hospital, I broke. Seeing her in such a situation made me realise that I wanted to protect her and that I loved her so much more than I cared about being snapped a time or two. I called her as soon as I could and begged her to come back, that I was ready to step into her world.'

He saw the woman before him melt at his romantic words and he knew she was going to write the piece that really did make him out to be a rough-around-the-edges Prince Charming. Women were going to be desperate to catch a glimpse of him. He wanted to smirk at the idea of telling Victoria such a thing later and seeing her response.

'I couldn't let him do that though,' Victoria said softly as she sat back up and partly extracted herself from his embrace. 'So, I met him in the middle. I've agreed to retire from royal life once we're married.'

'Wait,' the reporter said, her pen stopping as she processed Victoria's words. 'When did you propose?'

Cormac threw his head back and laughed. 'I didn't! Victoria proposed to me!' Maxine's eyes grew to the size of saucers as she stared between the two of them.

'I told you, I had to meet him in the middle. If he didn't want protocols in his life, then I'd throw them out of the window! Well, some of them,' she added with a smile. 'I'd just asked him to marry me the morning we got snapped for the first time at lunch.'

And that explained everything to the public—or at least the story they were telling. Cormac relaxed fractionally now that the lies were out there and let the discussion turn to their upcoming nuptials. There was little to say; after all, they didn't want to spoil the surprise of what her dress would look like or what flowers they'd have, for both their friends, family, and the general public who would be watching both across the nation and the world.

'Well, I have to say,' Maxine said, standing up and gathering her things as their time came to an end. 'I know we have some quick weddings in this country, but I am amazed a royal wedding was arranged so quickly.'

Victoria laughed. 'Not as fast as my uncle Harold's!'

The reporter considered her words with a tilt of her head and Cormac knew the woman was going to start looking up previous royal engagements and comparing them to theirs.

'It was lovely to meet you both,' the reporter said, stepping forward to offer her hand to each of them. She shook Victoria's first, who gave the woman a kiss on each cheek as a thank you, before she turned to Cormac. He shook her hand too and was slightly surprised when she held her cheek to him. He pressed a quick kiss to one cheek but hesitated as he pecked the second when she whispered, 'O'Malley isn't happy,' before stepping back with a bright smile.

As she left the room, Victoria escorting her to the sitting room door where Merryweather stood waiting, Cormac glanced down at the piece of paper she'd slipped into his palm.

With trembling fingers and a racing heart, he slowly unfolded the note and saw it was a telephone number.

'Well, I think that went well!' Victoria said turning to him with a wide smile.

'Yes,' he agreed, screwing up the paper before shoving it deep in his pocket. 'Very.'

She hurried to him with a spring in her step, and threw her arms around his waist, burying her head against his chest. He wrapped her in his embrace, glad she couldn't see his face as he tried to figure out what the hell he was going to do.

CHAPTER SIX

Victoria had never been one for crowds. Even knowing today's hordes were going to be there to support her—or to just catch a glimpse of the dress—on her big day, Victoria's anxiety tightened her chest and churned her stomach.

While *Chic* magazine had been kind and favourable to them in the only interview she and Cormac had given, publishing their cover story just as they told it, it hadn't stopped the rest of the media—or people desperate for likes on social media—taking snaps of them and reporting their every move. The few times they'd tried to go out and do normal things as a 'family' had ended in arguments and annoyance, Cormac feeling his life was being invaded and Victoria finally understanding what her cousins—especially Alistair—endured. Alexi, of course, had had no sympathy for them.

Luckily, they had spoken about the situations early, and towards the end of their engagement, while the days were still frustrating, they ended cuddled up together in bed rather than on opposite sides of the enormous mattress.

Victoria smiled at the memories of their nights. While not unskilled in the bedroom, she'd never experienced lovemaking the way Cormac made love to her. He made her body respond in ways no other man had ever been able to. She found herself completely desperate for him and aching in ways she hadn't realised existed, and he *always* left her completely satisfied.

But no matter how breathless he left her, no matter how much her toes curled, no matter how many times she literally touched heaven, she continued to crave him moments after they were finished. He was like a drug, and at twenty-five, perfectly able to keep supplying her however much she needed.

'Look at her,' Alexi sighed. Victoria watched her youngest sister in the mirror as she came up behind her, veil in hand. Hattie and Pippa were not far behind, each holding their own part of the insanely long lace. 'She's positively glowing.'

'She's radiant,' Pippa said with her own happy sigh.

'You do look happy, Victoria,' Hattie begrudgingly admitted. Victoria knew things would never be perfect between the two of them, but when it came to moments like this, she knew her sister would stand beside her.

'Thank you, Hattie, girls. I am. I really am,' she told them as the three began to affix the veil into her perfectly styled hair. 'I know you don't approve of how I've done this, but Cormac—he's everything I ever wanted and a few things I didn't realise I *could* have.'

'Do you love him?' Alexi asked, staring at Victoria's reflection in the mirror as she secured the lace in place. Victoria had to resist the urge to nod her head enthusiastically as her answer, not because she *did,* but because she *wanted* to love the man she was about to marry. And with that bouncing around inside her, she had no idea if the feelings that kept filling her chest every time she saw Cormac were real or just longings.

'No,' she answered, the fingers on her right hand, automatically going to play with her engagement ring, but it was missing today, ready for her wedding ring to go on unimpeded. 'But I believe I'm at risk of falling for him,' she admitted quietly. Her three sisters paused in their administrations and stared at her.

'Really?' Pippa asked.

Victoria bit her lip and nodded.

'Wow,' Hattie breathed. She stared at Victoria longer than the others and Victoria offered her sister a small smile in the mirror. 'Gimme that!' Hattie snatched the crown from Alexi's hands as her younger sister took it from the velvet-lined box.

Alexi relinquished it with raised brows but said nothing.

Hattie stepped in front of Victoria and carefully lifted the sapphire, diamond, and pearl piece up and settled it carefully onto Victoria's head, mindful of the hairstylist's work. It fit perfectly, almost as if it were made for her.

Victoria and her sisters had been left speechless that morning when the diadem had arrived. They'd expected several plainer and more modest *tiaras* to be sent for Victoria to choose from, never the *Tears of a Queen*. The piece was almost as old as the nation, sent by Queen Elizabeth—after she had taken the English throne from her sister Queen Mary—to Queen Jane as an apology for the way she had been treated under Mary's rule. It was a symbol of peace between the two nations, and one that the *Queens* of Avalone had worn throughout their reigns. No one save a ruling queen or queen-consort had ever worn it, and the four of them wondered how the world was going to take Victoria, a mere *lady* wearing the precious and delicate royal diadem.

But Victoria knew for certain that the King and the Grand Duke were going to burst a blood vessel when they saw her walking down the cathedral's aisle, the crown perched upon her head and glistening under the lights. Although, that might be her grandmother's plan.

'I'm sorry,' Hattie said, keeping her eyes on the delicate crown. 'For my reaction. For what I said. I shouldn't have called Cormac... well, *that*.'

There were so many petty things Victoria could have said to her sister; a tart reply of *no you shouldn't have* itched to slip from her tongue. Instead, Victoria smiled at her sister and as Hattie removed her hands, Victoria took the chance to grasp them and make her sister look at her. She squeezed Hattie's fingers gently in hers before saying, 'I forgive you.'

Tears swam in her sister's eyes before Hattie pulled her hands from Victoria's grasp and threw her arms around her.

'Careful!' Pippa cried in horror. 'You'll crease the dress!'

'Oh, get in here. All of you,' Victoria demanded happily as she clung tightly to Hattie, before laughing as all three sisters engulfed her at once for the first time since they were children.

Victoria didn't think she could feel more loved at that moment than if Cormac stormed in and declared his heart to her. She buried that thought somewhere deep inside herself. What they had was more than enough and right now, her family loved her enough to fill her heart.

∼

HARRY SIGHED AGAIN AS CORMAC TURNED ON HIS HEEL AND began another march across the room.

'Dude, you're making me dizzy!' Harry said as he watched Cormac's repetitive pacing. Cormac didn't stop as he glanced towards his best man. Harry looked positively green; to say he'd been surprised to be asked to be Cormac's best man was an understatement. After he'd recovered, he'd strutted around like a peacock, proclaiming he was going to get laid from now until forever based on this alone. But as the weeks went by—far too quickly in Cormac's opinion—the man had realised the seriousness of his role and that not only was the *whole world* going to be watching, but there would be kings, queens, princes, prime ministers, presidents, and countless other dignitaries actually *in* the cathedral and at the banquet afterwards. It wasn't the type of wedding Cormac would have wanted, but it was what Victoria's position demanded. Had she not been the first grandchild, they could have had the quiet, simple wedding they'd both talked about late at night under the safety of their bed covers.

'Where *is* he?' Cormac all but growled, running his hands through his hair in frustration. Harry huffing in irritation told Cormac he'd just ruined the look Nick had taken far too much time over.

'He'll be here. He's Head of the Royal Guard for crying out loud. He's probably got a dozen more important things to do than come for a chat at your whim.' Harry stepped up behind him and guided him to a chair to sit. He stared at Cormac, assessing the mess he had made of his hair, before trying to fix it. 'Besides, why you want to face your bride's ex-fiancé less than an hour before your wedding, I don't know.'

'You don't understand,' Cormac muttered. 'No one does.'

'Whatever, dude. Just don't blow this with less than an hour to go. Say the words and shag the bride *first* before screwing it up, so that you have to *divorce* rather than annul the wedding. *Big* settlement from that girl.'

Cormac shook his head, batting his friend away from him with his hands.

'What the hell, man?' he asked. 'I'm not running on Victoria.'

Harry threw his hands up before walking away. 'Fine,

look like you've been dragged through a hedge backwards in front of *billions* of people. It'll just make me look better next to you. And I didn't say you were; I said *screwing it up*,' he pointed out.

Cormac made to retort at his friend when there was a brisk knock on the door and Marcus poked his head inside.

'You asked to speak to me?' The Captain of the Royal Guard asked, looking between the two men glaring at one another.

'Yes!' Cormac stood up and bounced on his toes. The relief that ran through his veins was palpable. 'Harry, go take a walk, and come back just before we're due to leave.'

'What?' his friend asked, but Cormac simply opened the door wider to let Marcus in. He grabbed Harry's lapel and hauled him through the door.

'Take a walk.'

'Fine, fine,' Harry said, throwing his hands up as he turned and walked away. 'Worst time to come out, but whatever!'

'What?' Cormac and Marcus both said in confusion, looking at each other before turning to Harry, but the other man was already halfway down the hallway and waved at the stunned duo over his shoulder in dismissal.

'Please don't tell me you're gay,' Marcus pleaded at Cormac.

'I'm not bloody gay!' he cried as he slammed the door shut. 'I wish I were; that would be easier to resolve than the problem I'm in.'

'Ah, fuck,' Marcus sighed. 'I kinda liked you. I didn't want to have to kick your arse. Again.'

'Ha,' Cormac snorted. 'You'd need to grab a couple of other guys first.' The two men smiled, but Cormac's quickly fell. He turned to stare out of the window of the palace, seeing the people lining the streets trying to catch a glimpse of them as they went past. Cormac would leave in about half an hour to reach the cathedral fifteen minutes before Victoria, and in less than two hours, he was going to be a married man.

'So, d'you want to actually explain the problem?'

Cormac sighed, his shoulders sagging before he turned to the only man he thought might be able to help him.

'I want you to know that I'm only telling you this because the night we met, I saw that you still cared for Victoria.' He watched Marcus' whole demeanour change. 'I haven't asked Victoria why you two split up. I know it was you who ended it, and the way I saw you two together that night, I can't figure out why'—Marcus opened his mouth to speak—'but I don't *need* to know. All I need to know is that you'd do anything to protect her and keep her safe. Even if that means I walk out of here right now and disappear.'

Marcus' eyebrows almost flew off his head in surprise at his last words.

'Well, before you do that, perhaps you should tell me *why* you think you should? I did a full check on you and there was nothing in there. Not just a "nothing" that would cause alarm bells. I mean *nothing*.'

'I wonder if you'd find something if you did one right now?' Cormac shook his head to refocus himself. 'Look, I need to know if you'll do everything you can, even going above and beyond your position, to protect Victoria,' he repeated.

'I—' The man hesitated for a second, which surprised Cormac. 'I would,' Marcus finally said, although it was so quiet, Cormac might have missed it if he hadn't been listening.

'So, you *are* still in love with her?'

Marcus narrowed his eyes at him. 'I didn't end things because I stopped loving her,' Marcus snapped. 'And yes, I *love* Victoria, very much, but no, I'm not *in* love with her anymore. Now, how about you tell me what's got you so on edge—and I swear if it's just cold feet, I will shoot you myself!'

'Conner O'Malley.' Marcus' whole form went rigid at the name. 'He... He...' Cormac let out a frustrated growl and pulled at his hair again as he turned away from the other man. He squeezed his eyes shut as he finally confessed, 'He's blackmailing me.'

'How the hell did you get caught up with that dick?' Marcus asked. Cormac could hear him moving around behind him and jumped as a hand gently touched his shoulder. Marcus turned Cormac to face him.

'Tell me everything. And I mean *everything*.'

And so he did.

He explained how he'd never thought he'd hear from Victoria after the night they'd all met, that he'd turned the man down initially, but was in such dire straits he'd called him back. He confessed that Victoria had offered to marry him and help him out of the situation and that he'd lied to O'Malley instead of telling the truth and the threat that followed.

'Okay,' Marcus said slowly as he considered what Cormac had told him. 'I don't get it. You lied to him and then walked away. He has no idea that Victoria asked you to marry her—and we're going to circle back to *that*.'

'Nope. Her reasons are hers,' he told the Guard firmly. 'And I won't betray her confidence. But I also don't want her knowing that I considered that in the first place.'

'Whatever; explain *why* this is an issue now? How is he blackmailing you?'

Cormac rubbed his hands over his face as he told him that the reporter who'd interviewed them had slipped him a number.

'I was going to throw it away,' he confessed.

Marcus groaned. 'Please don't tell me you contacted it.'

'I didn't have to. After three days of me doing nothing, I got a message.'

'To *your* phone?' Cormac nodded. 'The mobile that *I* got Victoria for you?' Another nod, which made Marcus shake his head. 'No, that can't be. Those are sovereign phones. The devices are made to a set of specific specifications, they're on their own network, and each number is top secret. You must get permission to give out the number to anyone. A security check has to be done on them first.'

Cormac swallowed. 'But I have given it out—'

'To Miss Geri Clarke, Mr Harry Burton, Mr Nick Wilson, and a Mr Axel Bryans. They have all been checked and cleared for you to give the number to.'

'Wait, you'd already checked them?'

'As soon as Victoria requested a phone for you, we compiled a list of those that you'd probably give the number to. Those were the top names. And each of them has been advised that if that number is to be leaked to *anyone* for any reason, they will be arrested on charges of breaking the State's Secrets Act.'

'Whoa.'

'But we're now off topic. O'Malley sent you a message?' At Cormac's nod, Marcus held out his hand. 'Give it over.'

Cormac took it from his inside pocket and handed it straight to the guard.

'Before I open this, is there anything on it you don't want me to see?' Marcus asked with a raised brow. 'You know,' he added at Cormac's blank stare. 'Anything... *intimate*?'

'Whoa, dude, no!'

'Just thought I'd check.' The guard quickly assessed the outside of the phone—for what, Cormac had no idea. 'Pin number?'

'3-4-2-9.' He watched as Marcus typed it in and then continued to use the screen. He suspected the Guard was reading the message from O'Malley. Cormac could quote it. It wasn't difficult, just four little sentences.

You still have a debt to repay. I want dates and places you'll be. Nothing will happen to your new little family... Unless you don't comply.

He'd figured he'd be okay, that they had security around them whenever they went out, they lived safely tucked up at the top of a tower with some of the best security features in the country, and James would be transferring to a very private and elite school. There was no way anyone was getting to him there.

However, a second message had come in just that morning. A picture message.

'Where did they get the photo?' Marcus asked, glancing up at Cormac before pressing the screen. He held the device to his ear and looked at Cormac expectantly.

'It's a promotional shot they'd just had done at the club before I left.'

'How many are out there? Captain Walker here,' Marcus held up his finger at Cormac as he spoke to whoever had answered his called. 'Authorisation 2-0-7-5-Alpha-Tango-Romeo-Foxtrot-8-Oscar. I want a full scan on the device I'm calling from, and I want you to run a check on the number listed in this phone under question mark.'

Cormac went to say that it was under O'Malley, but Marcus shook his head at him. Had the guard changed it? Why? He rubbed his face as his mind whirled. This was all madness. It was like he was living in some insane movie or cheesy soap opera.

When Marcus finished his call, he turned back to Cormac.

'Okay, we'll deal with it. I want you to continue ignoring

any messages that come through to you. But when you do get one, I want you to send me a message—I've added my number—with nothing more than 7-7-7.'

'Why 7-7-7?' he asked.

'It's the number you call for information. It means you have information for— never mind, just type that to me, and *nothing* else, got it?' Cormac held up his hands and nodded. 'Okay, now how many pictures?'

'I don't know.' He took a seat as he tried to remember anything he could about the photoshoot they'd done just before he walked out. 'I never saw them save for on the photographer's laptop afterwards. They were done a few weeks before I left and were supposed to be ready before the new season started.'

'Season?'

'New dances introduced as the summer tourists roll in. I had assumed you guys had stopped all my promotional stuff from getting out there.' Marcus rubbed his hand over his mouth. Cormac shifted in his chair uneasily, under the man's weighing gaze.

'We thought so too. Do they have older ones of you? Could there be customers who have images of you?'

'No, phones were not to be out of the customer's bags. If they saw them taking pictures, Axel made damn sure they were deleted immediately. There were security cameras watching everything. And I was there less than six months. I missed the Christmas photos, thank God,' he added, recalling seeing pictures of Harry in a supposed *elf* costume. Apparently, he'd wanted to be Santa.

'Okay, leave it with me,' Marcus said. 'Right then, we have to get you to a wedding!'

'But don't you think—'

'I *think*,' the Guard said as he came over to Cormac and squatted down in front of him. The move made Marcus' jacket part and allowed Cormac to see the two guns he was carrying on either side of his broad chest. 'That we need to get you to your wedding.'

Cormac closed his eyes and swallowed before nodding his agreement.

'Cormac, do you want to know why I left Victoria?' Marcus asked, his voice softer than before. Cormac shrugged. Sure, he was curious, but he wasn't going to force anything from him.

'We met because I was part of the task force that went in to take out the thieves holding Victoria and the other customers hostage; you remember that right?' Cormac nodded. It had been ten years ago, and as a teen he'd watched it with mild interest, but that was all. He hadn't really thought about it until Victoria started explaining why security was so important.

'She got a bit of a crush on me'—the other man smiled as he recalled—'as I'd been the one to find her and protect her the whole time. We had to get her away from the other hostages just in case something went wrong.'

'A bit harsh,' Cormac said without thinking, but Marcus nodded.

'It's the way it works, unfortunately. So, she got a crush on me, and to be honest, I was quite taken by her. Eventually we decided to give it a go, but it was doomed from the start.'

'The King or her father?' Cormac asked, suddenly intrigued by why Marcus had walked away.

'Neither,' he confessed. 'There are rumours His Majesty made us split as I got promoted very quickly through the ranks after we separated, but that's not the case. After we ended, I threw myself into work. I'd actually been refused promotions beforehand in case it looked like favouritism.'

'So, you broke up with her for your career?'

Marcus shook his head. 'No, it's because I wasn't the man

for her. She loved the *idea* of me. The handsome guard who came to her rescue, who'd throw himself in front of her to save her life... But that was just part of my training. I didn't meet her in a gallant way, I saved her because it was my *job*. I'm trained to weigh up situations and avoid danger, not run headfirst into it. Yes, I'd take a bullet for her, but I'd do it for any one of her family because I'm *paid* to. I'm not the kind of man you are.'

Cormac blinked and sat back from the Guard as he tried to fathom what Marcus meant. 'What's that supposed to mean?'

Marcus sighed. 'I mean, if it came down to saving Victoria or saving the King today, who would you save?'

'Victoria.'

'You didn't even hesitate. *That's* why you're the man for her.'

'Wait, you—*Oh*.' Realisation suddenly dawned on Cormac as he comprehended what Marcus was truly saying.

'Yeah, I'm paid and trained to save the Crown. If it came down to it, I'd hesitate, and I honestly don't know what my answer would be. So as much as I loved Victoria—and still deeply care for her—I'll never be the man she wants. I can't say I'll always put her first.

'But you... you went for His Majesty, man!' Marcus said with a laugh as he stood up. 'I mean, c'mon! The fucking King!'

'I didn't even think.'

'Exactly,' Marcus said. 'That's why I know she's in good hands with you, regardless of... *this*.' He motioned between them, and Cormac took it to mean their conversation about O'Malley.

Taking a deep breath, he rose from his seat. Marcus glanced up at Cormac's hair when they stood face to face again.

'I think I need to go and get your friend before we get you to the cathedral.' He began to leave the room before pausing at the door. He didn't look back as he asked, 'I know how you guys really met and you say she proposed; do you love her?'

'I—' He didn't know. He enjoyed being with her and the sex... God, the sex was amazing. He'd never experienced anything like it before. But sex didn't equate to love, and their budding friendship didn't mean anything more than that. It didn't matter that when he looked over at her as she played a game on her phone and saw her little nose scrunched up with concentration, he smiled bright and wide. That his heart softened every time she gave him *that* smile. And just because he wanted to touch her *all* the time, to wrap her up in his arms, or kiss the back of her neck when she wore her hair up, it didn't mean that he was falling for her...

'I see,' Marcus said. Cormac saw the man's fingers flex against the door handle. 'Do you think you could?'

Cormac swallowed. 'Maybe?' he answered truthfully. If he was able to figure out exactly what love was, maybe he'd be able to love her.

'And the messages'—Marcus finally looked over at him —'don't worry about them. Remember to text me just as I told you and then carry on as normal. I have your back.'

As the Guard closed the door behind him, Cormac glanced out of the window and saw the crowds in the distance waving their little flags as a procession of horses walked along the boulevard he'd soon be driven down. He fell into the chair again, somehow feeling like a great weight had been lifted off his shoulders while simultaneously putting on some concrete shoes.

He just hoped he didn't wade into some water wearing them.

TAKING HIM

VICTORIA SMILED AND WAVED TO THE CROWDS AS SHE RODE through the city from the palace to the cathedral in the gold and glass carriage. She turned to one side and then the other, her smile wide and bright as it should be for any bride on her wedding day.

'Your face is going to be so sore tonight,' Alistair said opposite her, also smiling and waving, following her lead as to which side to pay attention to so the media could get them together. A strong and united front as the royal grandchildren finally grew up. But despite it being Victoria's big day, a lot of the media outlets were focusing on Alistair, whom she'd asked to give her away. He'd been delighted and rather excited at first, until the rumours started.

Will he be next down the aisle?

Will the Prince of Avalone find his bride soon?

Exclusive! The King ordered *Lady Snape to marry to get Alistair down the aisle next!*

The latter had been Victoria's favourite, especially because her cousin had come in and slammed the paper down, demanding to know if it was true. He'd been white as a sheet and Victoria hadn't been able to help the hysterical laughter that had bubbled up from her lips. She hadn't told him the truth of how she and Cormac had met and why she was being so quick about the whole wedding, but she had reassured him that the paper was lying and that she had no idea of any plots to get him married off anytime soon. His mother might be the actual reason for that, but Victoria kept mute on that point.

'Are you really happy?' Alistair asked as they switched sides.

'I am as happy as I can be,' she answered truthfully, hoping he'd take it to mean she was deeply in love and bought the story they'd sold everyone else as the truth. She glanced towards him when he didn't reply.

'I'm glad,' he finally admitted. They sat back in their seats for a few seconds as they went under a bridge. 'It gives me a little hope for my own nuptials.' Victoria felt her jaw drop.

'You're engaged?' she asked, agog.

'What? Hell, no!' he said, before putting his wide smile on again as they rolled back into the sunlight and more crowds. 'I'm going to avoid that as long as possible. I think Spencer has a pool running on how long I have left.'

'He does; I bet you'll be thirty-three. Cormac took thirty-eight. He's *so* going to lose.'

'You bitch.'

'Hey, Alexi said *she'd* be married before you, and you know she's looking to be a queen of somewhere. That's *never* going to happen, so that's something to hold onto.'

'Alexandra has *always* been my favourite.'

'She's betting thirty-one.'

'I hate you all. You're all dead to me. When I finally ascend to the throne, I'm cutting you all off.'

Victoria laughed heartily, throwing her head back and almost dislodging the diadem on her head.

'Careful now,' Alistair said, leaning forward to gently correct the weighty headdress. 'I still can't believe Grammy sent you *that*.' Alistair had stared at her completely dumbstruck when she'd walked out of her room at the palace, his eyes fixed on the *Tears of a Queen* upon her head.

And then he burst into laughter, a huge guffaw that brought tears to his eyes. She'd told him not to make a big deal out of it; it was simply the only one their grandmother had sent, and he'd just nodded, a wide smile on his face and a knowing glint in his eye.

'Well, this is it,' Alistair said, settling back in his seat as they turned onto the short road up the small hill that led to the Cathedral. 'Are you ready?'

She took a deep breath as she looked across at him. Her

cousin was going to have very little say in his own future, and while hers wasn't exactly what she'd wanted—or at least the way she wanted it to happen—she'd somewhat managed to have as much control over it as was possible.

'I am,' she said firmly as the carriage rolled to a slow stop.

Her sisters, all dressed in identical royal blue dresses, their hair coiffed to perfection, holding their small posies of flowers, stood at the bottom of the steps of the great building waiting for her. She smiled at them as Axel, in his role as usher, opened the door to the carriage. The roar of the crowd and the incessant ringing of the huge cathedral bells stopped Victoria in her movements as they deafened her. She fought the urge to slam her hands over her ears, but couldn't help the grimace on her face at the noise.

'Bloody hell,' she muttered as Alistair went before her, so he could help her get out with what felt like miles and miles of fabric pooling around her. 'I hadn't realised how well these carriages were insulated from the crowds.'

'I forget you don't get to enjoy all this splendour at the family get-togethers. Regretting not going for a prince now?'

'Oh, hell no! Now help me down.' Alistair laughed as he held out his hand and pulled her from her seat to help her climb out of the confining space. The yank he gave managed to get her out of the seat and she prayed the cameras behind them were kind to her as she knew they must have a great shot of her backside as she struggled to get down the three small steps without tripping on her gown. She'd wanted to arrive in a car, but it was *tradition* she arrive by carriage. Although, with the struggle she was having through the generous carriage doors, she didn't think she'd have been able to even fit *in* a car!

Her sisters hurried to get the dress back to the way it should be as the crowd behind them began to chant her name. As Hattie handed Victoria her bouquet, she turned to give the crowd gathered a wave, and the roar intensified.

'Victoria!' James' small voice caught her ear, and she smiled at the sight of her young almost brother-in-law. He was dressed in a child-sized military outfit as part of his pageboy regalia.

'Well, don't you look handsome!' she smiled and noticed that Alexi—who'd been put in charge of minding him—looking a little exasperated.

'I look like the dukes!' he said happily. 'Oh! And I got the rings, don't worry!' His little fingers fished inside the small hidden pocket on the breast of his uniform.

'It's okay,' she hastened to say to him in case he pulled them out and dropped them. 'Keep them there until Harry comes for them, okay?'

The little boy nodded his head eagerly and his searching fingers instead gave her a sloppy salute, which she returned with one of her own.

No doubt that image would be hitting the news sites immediately.

'Come on, Major Pain-in-my-Arse,' Alexi said with a sigh as she offered the child her hand again. 'Auntie Pippa said she's going to take care of you for a bit.'

Victoria couldn't help it; she laughed another good hearty laugh.

'Not so easy, is it?' she said to Alexi as they walked by. Her sister bit her lip and narrowed her eyes at Victoria, but she said nothing.

With her smile still lighting up her face, she took Alistair's arm, and the two began their ascent up the steps of the cathedral, slowly, so her sisters could straighten out the train of her dress and veil before they stepped inside the grand building.

'They're talking about the fact you're wearing *The Tears*,'

Alistair told her as he listened to the broadcast through a small earpiece. 'Apparently, it *is* a big deal.'

'You do have the medics on standby for when your father pops a vein, right?'

'No, and I'll bloody make sure *Doctor* George is held back by the Guard too.'

'Wow, Alistair, that's cold, even for you.'

The prince shrugged. She knew there was a rift between the Grand Duke and her cousin, but she hadn't thought it had reached the point of wanting each other dead.

'Hey, you have your happy thoughts for today to keep you smiling, and I have mine. Anyway, *who* do you think gave Grammy the idea to send you her masterpiece, eh?'

She turned to her escort, eyes wide and lips parted. 'You didn't.'

'Father was there when the Keeper of the Jewels arrived with a selection for her to choose which ones to send over to you. He *may* have been ranting about the audacity of you borrowing a tiara which annoyed Grammy so much, she actually made him leave. You know how she loves to look at the sparklies and he was clearly spoiling the atmosphere. But as he did, he made a flyaway comment about at least you wouldn't get to wear *The Tears*. *I* may have suggested to Grammy that it was a shame you wouldn't, because imagine his reaction if you wore it, especially before my mother did.'

Victoria burst out laughing. Their grandmother did have a bit of a spiteful streak, and it was no secret within the family that she did not like the arrogance her eldest son exuded. Victoria had even heard her mutter to her husband that he better live as long as possible to ensure Harold's reign was short. Not that Victoria would ever repeat that to anyone.

At least not again.

'Are you ready?' Alexi asked as they made it inside.

Victoria nodded. 'Nervous?' A shake of her head, before she paused and nodded instead. Her sister *tsked* as she looked up at the crown, the veil carefully in place over it until Cormac would lift it before their first kiss as man and wife.

As Alexi reached up to straighten it, Victoria admitted how she really felt with a whispered, 'I'm terrified.'

Alexi paused in her ministrations, her eyes far more serious than Victoria had ever seen them before.

'You don't need to be,' she whispered back. 'I've seen how he looks at you. You're both going to be very happy.'

'You— What?' But it was too late to question her sister further as the Dean approached with a wide smile on his face.

'Are you ready?' he asked. At her small nod, a blare of fanfares sounded, making her jump.

'Hey, you got this,' Alistair reassured her. She took a deep breath and nodded. Just before she moved forward, the errant thought that it should have been her dad walking her down the aisle popped into her head. She loathed that he'd done this to her, but also hated that he wasn't here to be part of her big day. She swallowed back the sudden lump in her throat and squeezed Alistair's fingers to tell him she was ready to step forward.

She hated that she had to walk the whole length of the biggest cathedral in the country. What she'd really wanted was a small ceremony in the secluded chapel at Renfrew Hall. Instead of a few steps to get to her husband-to-be, it was going to take her almost four minutes to walk the cathedral's aisle to the altar. The procession had been timed to perfection by her and Alistair. She'd insisted they walked it again and again that week just to make sure she wouldn't screw it up in front of the world.

Her step faltered as she remembered the dozens of cameras pointed at her at that exact moment, watching her every step and commenting on every facet about her. Was her dress too long or too short? Too plain or over the top? How was her hair and makeup; they didn't know that it drove Cormac mad when she wore her hair up—he always nuzzled her neck, sending shivers down her spine, before he loosened her hair so it would tumble about her shoulders.

'Hey, eyes on the prize, Victoria. Eyes on the prize,' her cousin whispered. 'Head up, smile, and focus on the man you love… Who appears to be breaking all the rules and is watching you.'

Victoria lifted her gaze and her eyes instantly found where Cormac was standing, still oh so far away. But Alistair was right, Cormac was facing the wrong way and was observing her journey to him.

She kept her eyes upon him and forgot about everyone and everything else around them as each step took her closer and closer to the man who had saved her life, her fortune, and who could very well save her heart.

As she finally arrived before Cormac, he held out his hand to her. She took a breath, handing her sister her bouquet and reached for his outstretched fingers.

And for a short time, no one else existed but the two of them and everything was perfect.

~

CORMAC HAD BEEN TOLD TO STAY STARING AT THE ALTAR, THAT it was tradition not to watch the bride walk down the aisle, that the first time he'd see her was when she was at his side. It was a stupid tradition, he'd thought, but had agreed to go along with it. After all, he was marrying into a family that had so many traditions and rules—far too many for him to recall—and while he didn't understand them all, it was important that he follow every one of them to the letter until the two of them were free of Victoria's title.

However, when the fanfare sounded and Harry nudged him, his eyebrows wagging suggestively as he leaned in and whispered, *Here comes the death march,* Cormac's eyes strayed from the altar to the north aisle at the side of where they stood. The choir's voices stirred and what sounded like heavenly music filled the ornate and grand cathedral, but he felt an overwhelming desire to *run*. He was sure he'd be able to make it to the exit he'd seen down the passageway when they'd been waiting for Victoria to arrive.

He jerked his shoulders, trying to loosen the muscles there; his jacket was too restrictive, it was hot and heavy, and the tie about his neck—a Trinity Knot just for Victoria—suddenly felt too tight. He couldn't breathe and it was slowly getting tighter and tighter.

Oh, God! He couldn't breathe!

He reached up to try and pull at the tie, but Harry's hand gently batted it away.

'Calm down, mate,' his friend said quietly. He saw the priest—maybe he was a bishop?—giving him the side-eye as the man tried to smile and watch Victoria walking down the insanely long aisle to them, but Cormac didn't care. He needed to leave! To get out of there. What the hell was he thinking? He couldn't *marry* into royalty! What the hell did he know about-

'Wow!' Harry gasped next to him. He'd turned around and was staring down to the west entrance where Victoria was walking from. 'Dude, I'm gay but with the way she looks right now, even I'd marry her!'

And Cormac distracted as he was, couldn't help it; he'd looked.

It was only supposed to be a quick flick of a glance over his shoulder, but he found his eyes lingering as a vision headed his way. The bishop-priest person *tsked* at him, but he didn't care. He felt himself turning, unable to look away from the angel walking towards him.

The dress was just… stunning, a beautiful ivory satin with a layer of delicate lace over it. Her flowers were simple, an arrangement of white and purple-blue blooms with fresh green foliage around them. Her long golden-brown hair was pinned up into what he guessed was a fancy chignon just above the nape of her neck and he felt the overwhelming urge he always felt when she wore her hair up, to set it loose about her shoulders so he could run his fingers through it—he loved it wild about her face as they made love.

And atop her perfectly made-up hair, just beneath the incredibly long veil that trailed behind her, was the most amazing crown he'd ever seen. It wasn't as fancy as some of the ones he knew the King and Queen owned, or other monarchs around the world, but the sparkling blue sapphires within their golden beds surrounded by a sea of diamonds and pearls twinkled under all the lights above them, giving her a sparkling halo to complete her angelic appearance.

He just wished she were looking at him. Instead, her head was slightly dipped, just enough to ensure she couldn't meet anyone's eyes, but high enough that the large ornate crown stayed atop her head. Her caramel eyes were fixed on the floor and he wanted to run up to her, to tilt her head up and tell her to keep it up, that she had no reason to hide away from people. That today was *her* day and she needed to *own* it.

And then she did.

Her eyes met his and his heart beat wildly for a reason so different than before.

'You are so smitten,' Harry whispered in his ear, and Cormac couldn't stop himself from nodding. He was caught in the same feeling he'd had the night he'd met her, that feeling that no one else existed, that in that moment there were only the two of them. Except this time, it didn't last for just a second.

She finally reached him and he held out his hand. She gave her flowers to someone behind her before placing her fingers atop of his. He held them gently, pulling her towards him and as she stood at his side, his lips spread into his crooked smile.

'You look... amazing,' he told her, his gaze unwavering

'You scrub up pretty well yourself,' she replied, that heart-melting smile gracing her lips. Lips he just wanted to capture in a kiss, but the stupid veil was in the way. He lifted it and Victoria's breath hitched at the action, making his smile widen, knowing she wanted him as much as he wanted her.

'Ahem!'

Cormac blinked and glanced over Victoria's shoulder to where the noise had come from.

Prince Alistair stared at him. His brows were raised, but it was merriment that filled his piercing blue eyes.

'That was supposed to be done later, when we're man and wife and just before you kiss me,' Victoria whispered as she gazed up at him through her long, dark lashes. He heard Harry snigger behind him, but it was the Archbishop *tsking* at him *again* that made his cheeks flame red.

'What if I want to kiss you now?' he asked, trying to ignore the judging man waiting for them.

'Marcus might have his men tackle you to the ground again.'

'Aww, we wouldn't want that—I'd wrinkle.' Victoria giggled and squeezed his fingers. 'I suppose I have to marry you first then?'

'I'm afraid it's the only way.'

'Ah, well, I suppose I could manage. I have the fancy suit after all.'

Victoria's eyes glanced down, taking in his appearance, her gaze settled on his elaborate tie before her smile widened and her eyes returned to his.

'You remembered I had a penchant for this knot.' Her eyes flickered to the Archbishop before she leaned in and whispered, 'I'm going to enjoy getting you out of that later.'

'Yeah? Well, wait until I get my hands on that hair of yours.'

She bit her lower lip to stop whatever reply wanted to slip from her tongue as the music came to an end and the Archbishop began to speak, forcing them to turn and give their full attention to the man who was to marry them.

'Dearly beloveds...' Cormac listened to the words with half an ear. They would be broadcast throughout the world, and he'd be able to watch them again and again thanks to the likes of YouTube and RoyalHouseholds.net—he had to thank Geri for telling him about the latter—if he really wanted to hear all the religious stuff. Instead, he kept glancing towards Victoria, meeting her gaze once or twice, and the two of them smirked and smiled at each other like loved-up teenagers.

'...confess it now, if you know of any lawful reason why you both should not be joined in Holy Matrimony.' The words called Cormac's attention back to the man before them. A few hours ago, those words would have torn him apart, he realised. But in that moment, he recognised the worry he'd been feeling that morning had evaporated the second Victoria stepped into view.

'Cormac Dean, will thou have this woman as thy wedded wife? Will thou love her, comfort her, honour, and protect her, and, forsaking all others, be faithful to her as long as thou both shall live?'

Cormac took a deep breath. An ache suddenly formed deep within him; they weren't in love and certainly didn't plan on the whole *until death do they part* bit of the marriage vows, but he would ensure that he kept the rest of the vows completely.

'I will,' he said confidently, loud enough for those nearest to him to hear. And certainly loud enough for the microphones hanging everywhere to pick up.

'And you, Victoria Georgina, will thou have this man as thy wedded husband? Will thou love him, comfort him, honour, and protect him, and, forsaking all others, be faithful to him as long as thou both shall live?'

She didn't even hesitate. 'I will,' she replied and looked at Cormac, happiness glistening in her eyes. The ache inside him slowly subsided as he saw something within her that spoke to him, that told him perhaps they *could* make good on every single word they agreed to today.

Suddenly, that didn't seem like such a strange concept, that a woman he'd only known for two months could be someone he wanted to spend the rest of his life with.

'Who gives this woman to be married to this man?' the Archbishop asked, looking around as if he couldn't see Alistair standing next to Victoria. Cormac resisted the eye roll, only because he knew the cameras would be completely focused on them during this part. No cuts to the congregation—most of whom couldn't even see them tucked away in the wings of the building!

'I do,' said Alistair, taking Victoria's hand again and handing it over to the Archbishop who immediately handed it to Cormac. Neither of them had liked this part and had asked if it could be removed seeing as Victoria was her own person and was no one's to *give away*. But it had been refused, and Victoria swore up and down that it was her grandfather and uncle who had refused them. It was one of the many reasons why she'd chosen Alistair to walk her down the aisle. She'd give neither of the other men the satisfaction of the task.

Cormac turned to Victoria and—as they'd agreed—said his vows without the bishop having to say them first. It would make the crowds outside and the public watching at home go wild, thinking they were so in love to recite their vows perfectly, having committed them to their hearts.

'I, Cormac Dean, take thee, Victoria Georgina, to be my wedded wife, to have and to hold from this day forward, for better, for worse, for richer, for poorer; in sickness and in health; to love and to cherish, till death us do part, according to God's holy law; and thereto I give thee my troth.'

He'd had to look up what troth meant: faithfulness, honesty, loyalty. He had no problem with the first and last part, but it had been the second—*honesty*—that had made him want to bolt that morning.

Victoria gazed up at him, her eyes filled with truth and feeling as she spoke her own vows. Her face alight with happiness as the words fell from her lips without a stutter or even a hint of hesitation, and if Cormac hadn't known that the marriage wasn't one filled with love, he'd have been completely taken in, believing that she was totally and utterly devoted to him, and this truly was the happiest day of her life.

'Do you have the rings?' the Archbishop asked. The two turned towards where her sisters sat with James tucked safely between Pippa and Alexi. The two Snape Ladies encouraged him off his chair and to step forward.

'He looks so smart,' Cormac whispered as his little brother slowly but purposefully climbed the steps that led to them. Harry stepped over to meet him near the top and dipped his head as James whispered something to him. Harry nodded and reached into James' little pocket, struggling a little to get to the rings. The congregation whispered, and

Alistair, still at Victoria's side, glared at the lot. Cormac saw the Grand Duke snort and promised to make sure the arrogant dick got his nose rubbed in the rest of the day as much as possible, even if Cormac had to ham it up even more.

Harry finally got the rings and patted James on the head before ruffling his hair. James scowled at the action and batted away his hand, causing a little ripple of amusement in the front few rows.

'Sorry, apparently the pocket was too deep for his fingers to reach them,' Harry told the pair as the bishop—who looked far from amused—held out his hand.

'Heavenly Father, by your blessing let these rings be to Cormac and Victoria a symbol of unending love and faithfulness, to remind them of the vow and covenant which they have made this day through Jesus Christ our Lord.'

The crowd responded with *Amen*.

The bishop handed a ring to Cormac. He took Victoria's hand in his and she bit her lip to try and control her smile as he brought the simple, slim band of rare Welsh gold—a gift from the British Royal Family—up to her ring finger. He held her excited eyes as he spoke.

'Victoria, I give you this ring as a sign of our marriage.' He cleared his throat before he continued. 'With my body I honour you, all that I am I give to you, and all that I have I share with you, within the love of God, Father, Son and Holy Spirit.

'I know I haven't brought as much to this marriage as you have, financially.' He had no idea why he spoke the unscripted lines, but he felt a burning need to say them there and then in front of everyone. Victoria blinked at the unexpected addition, but other than that, no one would have thought it wasn't a planned part of their ceremony.

'But I promise, with everything in my being, that I will cherish you, protect you, and ensure that I always bring a smile to your lips. That any children we share will always feel loved, wanted, and needed in our lives. I promise to always be there for you, to stand by your side through every hardship and heartache, and be your support when you are tired and weary.' He wanted to say so much more, but the tears shimmering in Victoria's eyes brought a lump to his own throat. 'These things I pledge to you with all my being,' he managed to finish.

She smiled up at him, nodding her head as she fought back the tears that threatened to fall down her cheeks. He reached up, gently cupping her face and brushed at her lashes with his thumbs to wipe them away. She held onto his wrists so tightly and he could see she was desperate to say something to him but couldn't, due to the ceremony.

When he dropped his hands, she took his in hers and the bishop handed her the ring he'd wear—not Welsh gold, but rich Avalonian.

'Cormac, I give you this ring as a sign of our marriage. With my body I honour you, all that I am I give to you, and all that I have I share with you, within the love of God, Father, Son and Holy Spirit.' She pushed the ring onto his finger and then met his gaze again. He smiled wide, encouraging her to break the tradition herself and speak up.

'I—' Her voice broke. 'You say I bring more to this marriage *financially*, but you have given me so much; you have protected me against all others, raised me up within my own eyes, and held me as the most precious gift in the world, something which no other has ever done. I promise to you that you will never feel wanting, you will never feel you are unequal, and that you will always stand beside me in all that we do *together*. I promise that our children will never fear a lack of love or understanding in their lives as we raise them as one. I promise these things to you with all of my being.'

She smiled at him, and Cormac felt his breath catch in his

throat as her beautiful eyes showed the depth of her passion and feeling for him.

He had no idea if she knew it, but within her eyes he saw her *love* for him.

'In the presence of God, and before this congregation,' the Archbishop said, supposedly to call their attention back to him, but Cormac couldn't look away from Victoria. She loved him, deeply and completely. She was, as Harry accused him earlier, utterly smitten.

'Cormac and Victoria have given their consent and made their marriage vows to each other. They have declared their marriage by the joining of hands and by the giving and receiving of rings.' The bishop didn't mention that they had committed their *love* for one another. Just their *consent*. But that was because they weren't in love... or they weren't supposed to be.

'I therefore proclaim that they are husband and wife. Those whom God has joined together let no one put asunder. You may now kiss the bride.'

Victoria's eyes brightened at the words, her smile widening in happiness and excitement. Cormac leaned forward and lightly brushed their lips together as they had practised. As he slowly pulled away, the congregation applauded and Cormac saw her dark lashes still against her cheek, a sigh slipping from her lips, and in that moment, he knew that he loved her. With everything he had, he loved Victoria Georgina Blake.

He kissed her again, gathering her up into his arms and branding her as his with his lips for all the world to see. She gasped against his mouth, but melted into his body, wrapping her arms around his neck and deepening the kiss. A roar rose from outside as the crowds saw them on the giant television screens across the city.

When they finally broke apart, he pressed his forehead to

hers and returned her smile. He'd keep his feelings a secret for now, unwilling to have them used against him. If she wasn't aware of her own heart, he didn't want to suffer an injury to his in trying to get her to see what was between them.

'Ready, my *wife*,' he whispered.

'Yes, dear *husband*,' she giggled, before she threw her head back and smiled brightly up at the ceiling, unable to contain her happiness any longer.

Cormac never wanted her to.

CHAPTER SEVEN

Cormac leaned against the railing of the balcony overlooking the immaculate gardens of the Grand Palace as the party continued in the Yellow Ballroom. Some guests milled about, talking quietly in pairs or small groups as they took respite in the cool night air.

Just a few hours before, he'd been on a different balcony, the crowds cheering and waving, chanting their names before demanding their kiss—which he and Victoria had obliged them with. When they'd come in, they'd been whisked off for their official wedding photographs with the King and Queen, Grand Duke and Duchess, and Alistair surrounding them. Only then had they been allowed a few shots of their own choosing.

Victoria had later told him there would be a second photographer roaming about the lunch and evening party, taking more relaxed images of them and their guests. He hadn't noticed anyone snapping away, but then again, he'd met so many people in the receiving line, he may well have missed them. He'd actually lost count of the number of hands he'd shaken and bows he'd made, and he swore if he had to try and pronounce the name of the Japanese emperor—who seemed to want to become his best friend because of his inability to say the man's name—once more, he was going to throttle someone.

'Oh. My. God!' Geri bounded over to him. Her face filled with excitement and delight, told him she was bursting to tell him something and there was no way he was getting out of it. She stopped right at his side, grinning at him like a loon as she clapped her hands with the enthusiasm of a child.

'There are no blue seals as far as I'm aware,' he said, standing back upright and turning to her. He took a sip of his brandy he'd been nursing before adding, 'Now, blue whales on the other hand...'

'Right now, I'm going to ignore that you called me fat because do you *know* who I was just talking to?' she said, unfazed by his comments.

He took a breath and let it go in a long huff as he searched for someone preposterous. He went to say Queen Edith, the Queen of England, but then remembered she was *actually* at the party. And her husband and son. And she wasn't called the Queen of *England*, she was Queen of the United Kingdom of Great Britain and Northern Ireland... plus a dozen or so other countries. At least he hadn't spoken that little slip during the reception line; Victoria would have elbowed him... Just as she had when he'd called the King of Holland the King of the Netherlands. Or was that the other way around?

'I dunno.'

'Oh, c'mon. Guess!' she pleaded. 'You did just call me fat, you owe me.'

'I *didn't* call you fat. And I thought you were ignoring that.'

She shook her head and narrowed her eyes at him. 'Guess,' she demanded.

'Celine Dion.'

Geri's eyes went wide. 'No! Is she here?' She turned and made to walk back inside before he grabbed her arm to stop her darting off.

'No, she's not here.' Or at least he didn't think so. There were so many people he supposed she *could* be. 'Just spill.'

'Lady Philippa Snape!'

Cormac frowned. That was a big deal to his smurfy friend? If he'd have known that, he'd have dragged her to Pippa weeks ago!

'Yeah, she's Victoria's sister.'

'I know! But, I mean, c'mon!'

Nope, Cormac did not understand. 'You do know that you're in *the* Grand Palace, right? Surrounded by kings and queens. You remember meeting Prince Alistair a few weeks back? He complimented your hair.'

'Yeah, I know,' she said, waving him off. Her eyes drifted off towards the gardens for a moment and he swore a tint of pink hit her cheeks, but before he could question it, her mouth was running again. 'And trust me, *that's* also amazing. *But* Lady Philippa is a *goddess* in the financial world. A *genius!*'

'Hattie's smarter apparently,' Cormac commented over the rim of his glass before he took another sip.

'Yes, but Lady Philippa—'

'Pippa.'

'—created the accountancy software that almost *every* major company has switched over to. *We* use *2+2*'s software! It's amazing. So easy to use and saves us *so* much time and—'

'I thought she was, like... an *actual* accountant?'

'Well, she *is*,' Geri agreed. 'But she realised that there were so many laws, rules, and regulations, and the fact that they change from country to country meant that there needed to be an easier way of handling things globally, so she created-'

'Geri, are you seriously this excited over a piece of software?'

'I am about the woman *behind* it and that she told me to come for an interview next week!' She bounced up and down on the spot again, clapping her hands excitedly.

'She did?'

'*Yes!*' she squealed. 'Do you know what this could mean for me? No more working until four in the morning, counting up and running the numbers after oiling up guys or fluffing them before their big dance. I could work in a *real* accountancy firm, doing a *real* accountancy job!'

'Ah, I'm happy for you,' Cormac said, and he genuinely meant it. Geri had a natural knack with numbers, but with the way she looked, very few companies would give her a chance. He hated that she was left giving guys a quick hand job in return for being allowed to do a job she really wanted to do. Even if it was only the basic bookkeeping stuff.

He raised his glass to his friend before knocking the remaining brandy back in one gulp.

'Are you okay?' Geri asked. She pursed her lips as she considered him through her blue fringe.

'I'm tired. This day was supposed to be about me and Victoria.' He sighed as he turned back around to the view beyond the garden walls. The moon sparkled off the ocean in the distance, and Cormac yearned for the freedom it offered.

'Er, that's what this party is for, is it not?' his friend asked. She joined him at his side, mimicking his position by resting her elbows on the balustrade as she turned to admire the view. 'And if I'm not mistaken, it was *your* face gracing TV screens around the world earlier on. *Your* lips locking that made the city go mental. Apparently, you could hear the cheers from miles away. Although I suppose every place was probably doing the same thing.'

That was still a crazy thought. Cormac Blake, who'd kept

his head down, his nose clean, and had strived not to leave a digital fingerprint anywhere, was probably the world's most famous man today. Victoria promised that in a few weeks, he'd go back to being someone that people wouldn't remember. He'd scoffed at that, but she'd reassured him he'd take on the air of someone people would think they'd seen before but couldn't quite place. He decided he'd happily accept that if he could have it.

'That's the thing, our moment was then, but *this*'—he pointed over his shoulder back towards the ballroom—'isn't for us, it's for *him*.'

'Ah.' Geri nodded her head in understanding. She knew his feelings on the King and the way the family treated Victoria and her sisters. 'I see.'

They watched in silence as an ocean liner's silhouette appeared between the moon and its bright reflection in the water. After a few minutes, Geri asked, 'So why don't you guys just leave?'

'Because—'

'You've greeted the guests, listened to the toasts, done the dance, cut the cake, spoken to about a gazillion people—'

'And you want to be an accountant.'

'Ignoring you. You've done *everything*. All Victoria has to do is—'

'Throw the bouquet.' Victoria's voice startled them. She stood there smiling at them both. 'We can do it in about ten minutes; then we're free to leave.'

'That'd be nice,' he said, taking her in again. After the photographs and before the party, she'd changed into a second dress—which had caught him by surprise. It was a beautiful silky thing that he just wanted to run his hands over. It was still ivory in colour, but shorter and thus easier for her to walk and dance in. But it made her look less princessy, which he found a little disappointing. Although the fact she still had the *Tears of a Queen* perched on her perfectly coiffed hair made him smile.

She'd told him her grandmother had waltzed into the room just as she was about to walk out without any form of tiara and *demanded* she put it back on. Married women weren't supposed to walk about at formal occasions with a naked head, apparently. Another weird rule he didn't understand, but she looked amazing and he found himself telling her so.

'Thank you,' she said, dropping her gaze slightly. She blushed at his compliment and he couldn't help the smile that came from knowing he could make a woman of her stature flush like a teenage girl meeting her crush for the first time.

'I'm just gonna... Yeah,' Geri said, pointing to the doors that led back inside before disappearing. Cormac only saw her move from the corner of his eye because he couldn't tear his eyes from his *wife*.

It was still surreal to think that he was a married man. And even though they'd only met eight or nine weeks ago, it felt like an eternity. He knew there was so much to still learn about the woman in front of him, but he also felt like he'd known her forever.

'You look rather good yourself,' she told him as she stepped closer. 'And that tie of yours...'

'This little thing?' he teased, his hands reaching up to adjust it slightly. Her eyes dropped to watch his fingers caressing the silk, and he grinned as her tongue slipped out over her lips to wet them. He'd specifically asked his valet that morning to create the insanely intricate knot, hoping it would have just such a reaction. 'You like it?'

'I suppose.' She shrugged her shoulders as she tried to look nonchalant, but he could see that she really wanted to touch it. 'Although,' she paused and bit her lip, looking up at him through her lashes. He wanted to haul her to him, devour her mouth with his as he ran his hands up her legs, pushing up her skirt to—

'—I think it would look better on the bedroom floor.'

He growled as he reached out and grabbed her waist, hauling her against his wanting body. She gasped at the action, her hands falling against his chest to steady herself, but her eyes were brought level with his tie. Her fingers inched towards it, slowly, as she bit down on her lip and glanced up at him.

'If you're not careful, princess,' he said, his voice deep and gravely as he tried to keep control of himself. 'I'm going to make love to you out here, up against this railing.'

'Promises, promises,' she whispered huskily.

'How long do we have to stick around for?'

She glanced at the diamond encrusted watch on her wrist. 'Another five minutes before I throw the damn flowers.'

'What are we going to do for five minutes?' he said as he lowered his head towards hers. She sucked in a breath, thrusting her small but perfect breasts out and Cormac found himself dropping his forehead to hers, closing his eyes tightly and biting down on his own damn lip. She mewed a little in protest, but he knew that if he kissed her now, he wouldn't stop.

The music inside had changed since she'd come out, a slower melody playing as the band began to wind down.

'Dance with me,' he whispered.

'What?' she replied, her voice filled with confusion. Unable to step away himself, he gently pushed her back a step so he could hold out his hand to her properly.

'May I have this dance?' he asked. She glanced between his upturned palm and his enquiring face before she carefully reached out and placed her hand in his. He walked her towards the ballroom but stopped halfway to the state room and turned to face her. He dropped her hand before bowing to her deeply and standing again. She stared at him questioningly, before lowering herself into a curtsey.

He smiled and held out his hand again, when she took it, he pulled her into a perfect frame and began to move. She moved with him effortlessly, instantly following his steps as if the two of them had danced this way a thousand times before, but her befuddled face told a different story. They'd only practised one dance together, a formal waltz he'd been told was the traditional first dance of Avalonian royal couples. She had no idea he'd been secretly learning the tango to surprise her at some point.

It wasn't overly complicated, but the twists and turns made it look dazzling and dramatic. She gasped as he pushed her away only to pull her back to his body, holding her close before dipping her low.

She smiled as he spun her, stopping her with her back to his body, his hands sliding down her slight curves before grabbing her hips and turning her sharply to him. She landed against his chest just as the music calmed again and it allowed them to take a few standard steps.

'The tango?' she said a little breathlessly. 'I'm guessing Tonya taught you this as well?'

He laughed. 'Yes, I wanted to surprise you.'

'But the *tango*?'

'What? If Arnold Schwarzenegger and Al Pacino can do it, it's probably the coolest dance you can learn, right?' he said with a shrug before he whisked them across the balcony in a series of turns.

'I knew I shouldn't have insisted on a nineties film night!' she said with a laugh as she rolled away from his body before being pulled back to him again. He knew his moves weren't as complicated or as proficient as those in the films, but he was glad they brought a smile to her lips. Perhaps with some more practise, he could lead with just a single hand on the small of her back and do one-handed dips with her, like Arnie had in *True Lies*. She'd be able to do fancy kicks and drop down his body before slowly sliding back up his—

A soft round of applause caused him to stumble in his step and the two stopped dancing, immediately turning to see their guests gathered at the now fully opened windows that separated the ballroom from the balcony. The King and Queen stood front and centre of the crowd, their hands gently clapping what was meant to be a private moment between him and Victoria.

He wanted to snarl and snap at the crowd, to tell them they had no right to intrude on *this*. They'd been witness to almost everything else that day between himself and Victoria —including witnessing his realisation that he *loved* the woman in his arms—couldn't they just have *this*? But instead of yelling at the lot of them to piss off, he forced a smile to his face, pulled Victoria in closer, and nodded to the group as they began to disperse.

'Victoria!' Alexi said, hurrying over with the bridal bouquet in hand. 'Sorry to have spoilt your dance'—well, at least *someone* recognised when they weren't wanted—'but it's time to throw the bouquet.'

'We're all dying to know who's next!' shouted Blair, one of Alexi's friends.

'Want to know if you'll land one of the princes here?' Victoria asked her sister with a giggle, which Cormac found rather adorable. 'There's a number of heirs to a few thrones here for you to pick from this evening.'

Alexi rolled her eyes. 'I already *know* which country I'm going to be queen of,' she said with such conviction, Cormac wondered if she was already engaged and was the next to be announced.

'Really?' Victoria scoffed. 'And which one is that?'

'You'll have to wait and see, just like everyone else.'

Victoria snorted a noise of disbelief at her sister's proclamation.

'Come on already!' Francesca, one of Victoria's cousins shouted. 'Throw the damn thing!'

'Okay, gather round!' Victoria said before glancing up at him. 'If you have your phone, I suggest you film this. It's *so* going to be worth it!' He frowned before fishing his device from his pocket as all the single women gathered in front of the doors a good few feet from Victoria. A number of men that had separated from the earlier crowd had stepped to the side to watch the spectacle and were already holding up their phones to capture the moment.

Victoria turned her back to the group. 'Three, two, *one!*' she shouted before letting go. The group of girls squealed and shouted as they watched the arch of the bouquet and all began to clamber towards where they thought it would land. The men around began to laugh as the flowers hit the group and a mad scramble was made by the women. Cormac had the brief thought that a rugby scrum was far more civilised; elbows were flying, nails were out, and the noise... God, he thought being tortured might be more humane!

'They're hers!' He heard Alexi scream as she pulled one woman away from another by their hair. He winced at the thought, but couldn't stop watching for love nor money, wondering who the hell had managed to succeed securing the delicate posy in such a mess.

'Let go!' Blair shouted, as she bodily forced two or three other women away from the centre of the commotion. Victoria watched with hands to her face as the winner was heaved up off the *floor* by two other women.

'Hattie?' she breathed as she watched the third Snape sister stagger to her feet. Her dress was crushed and crumpled, her headdress of flowers was completely skewed—there was certainly no saving it as had been planned—and Cormac thought her lip looked a little swollen. She certainly looked dazed as she stood there staring at the bashed blooms as if she had no idea what they were and how she had come by them.

The men at the side-lines cheered and one man came along, hand out, fingers waving as he collected his winnings from his fellow spectators.

'They pulled names from a hat earlier,' Victoria told him as Alexi and Pippa helped Hattie limp back inside. He hoped they got her a *very* stiff drink. '*Please* tell me you got every single moment of that?' He glanced down at his phone to see it still focused on Hattie just as the curtain was pulled back over the windows. He nodded. 'Nice. I want to watch it again and again and again—do you *know* how many of them I've been in?'

He hadn't thought of that.

'Ever been the one to catch it?'

She shook her head. 'I never really tried for it. To be fair, I don't think Hattie did though either, she was just caught in the middle. I've seen women lose teeth before today in one of them.'

'Seriously?'

She tapped her left incisor. 'Blair, Alexi's friend, took an elbow to it about two years ago at Vanessa Smyth's wedding.'

'Bloody hell.' He stared at the small groups of women that were left, fixing each other's dresses and hair, and trying to look as if they hadn't just participated in the free for all, before they ventured back inside. 'Does this mean we can go now?'

'Oh, yes,' Victoria said, pressing herself against him as he wrapped her in his arms again. 'And as soon as we get to our room, I want you to do everything you were thinking of doing to me earlier—we've got our own private balcony after all.'

∽

VICTORIA HELD CORMAC'S HAND TIGHTLY AS SHE DRAGGED HIM through the maze that was the palace's hallways. All night she'd been pulled this way and that, yet it always seemed to be in the opposite direction from her new husband. She had been spun around the palace's biggest ballroom in the arms of almost every man save for the one she really wanted, and now that she was free of her grandfather's timetable, she wasn't going to waste another minute.

She wanted her husband, had been desperate for him from the moment she'd seen that damn tie he'd worn in the church. And that kiss... It had not only sent her knees week, but melted every bone in her body. She'd forgotten about everyone and everything and had never wanted it to stop.

If it wasn't for the fact that anyone could come walking through one of the hallways at any moment, she'd have pushed Cormac up against the nearest wall and had him take her there and then. Her breath quickened at the thought and her step faltered at the idea of doing such a thing.

'...you sure?' a male voice whispered from around the corner she was about to take. Victoria jerked to a stop and took a step back. Cormac wrapped his arms around her and held her close as they paused, holding their breaths as they tried to hear who it was.

'Oh God, I've never done this be— Oh!'

Victoria's eyes grew wide in the dim hallway as she recognised the hushed voice. To others it would have been difficult to discern, but he'd whispered secrets to her so often that it could only be one person—Alistair.

'Don't— Don't stop,' her cousin whispered heatedly

before letting out a long guttural moan that straddled the line between pleasure and pain. Victoria slapped her hand over her mouth, unsure if she was stopping a burst of laughter or an exclamation of disgust at catching the perpetual virgin prince in flagrante.

She looked up at Cormac who stared down at her with amusement in his eyes. He raised his brows, asking if they were going to drop in on the lovers, but Victoria shook her head. They were definitely *not* gate-crashing whatever first time experience her cousin was embarking upon. Instead, she unwound herself from her husband's grasp and quietly lead him in the opposite direction, going the long way to their room, and hoped no-one else decided to retire early that evening. Alistair's pornographic moans followed until Victoria deemed them safe enough away to run at full pelt, giggling the whole time.

'Who was that?' Cormac asked, whispering even though they were too far for the clandestine couple to hear them.

'Alistair,' she laughed. 'Finally getting his rocks off.'

'Finally?' But Victoria shook her head. It wasn't right to discuss her cousin's problems, and discussing the lack of Alistair's sex life was definitely not going to set the mood she wanted.

Especially as they'd finally managed to reach their room.

She hurriedly unlocked the door and slipped inside, pulling Cormac in with her by his lapel. He'd barely closed the door behind them when she was on him, a desperate need within her to claim his lips again. He kissed her back with a fervour, gathering her up in his arms.

'Tell me,' she said, huskily, when Cormac broke the kiss to trail his lips down her throat. 'What you were thinking of on the balc—' Her words were cut off as he pressed his lips to the juncture between her neck and shoulder, making her gasp in pleasure as he bit down just a little.

'I was thinking,' he murmured as his hands finally found the zip of her dress. 'Of how I'd have bent you over the railing, gathered your skirt up around your waist, pushed your knickers to one side'—Victoria groaned as desire flooded through her at the image—'and just made love to you there and then.'

She'd thought it to0, had pictured it so clearly, and it had turned her on more than anything else she'd ever thought of before in her life.

'Stop,' she whispered as his fingers inched the zip of her dress lower.

'What?' Cormac lifted his head, his eyes dazed, and confusion written on his face as his fingers stilled. His befuddlement only grew as she stepped back, out of his grasp, reaching behind her to wiggle the zip back up into place. One step turned into two, and then another as she walked further and further into the palace's wedding suite and towards her new goal.

'I want *that*.'

'Victoria, what are you—'

'I told you, we have our own balcony.' She hoped he got her meaning as she turned and hurried to the large glass doors hidden behind the ridiculously heavy curtains. She found the door's handle and pushed it open; the cool night air whispered through the room and enticed Victoria to go outside.

She turned back, a smirk upon her lips as she crooked her finger and beckoned Cormac to follow her.

As soon as the curtain fell shut behind her, she quickly unzipped her dress and shimmied out of it, before kicking it away into the corner. She hurried to the balcony's railing and positioned herself before it, dressed in just her ivory bra, satin French knickers, white stockings, stiletto shoes, and the *Tears of a Queen* still atop her head.

When she was finally where she wanted to be, she rested her hands on the stone balustrade and stared out into the night.

The moon hung low in the clear August sky, lighting up the landscape in an otherworldly glow. The quiet calm of the gardens stretched before them and beyond that the silent waters of Davenpool. Usually, the deep bay was a blanket of darkness stretching out towards the distant city of Daven on the other side of its banks. But tonight, it shimmered under the moon's brightness, making it seem as if the ocean itself held the stars within its grasp.

The picture was accompanied by the soft melodies of the orchestra still playing at the party below. Their notes drifting out into the darkness and Victoria imagined them being swept up into the night sky and becoming the stars that shone the brightest.

'Princess, I don't— Whoa!'

She had to bite down on her lip to stop the smirk stretching across her face. Instead she offered her new husband a coy little glance over her shoulder before turning her attention back to the visage before her.

'Fuck, Victoria.'

The way he muttered it, she knew it wasn't meant to reach her ears, but she couldn't help but use it to her advantage. As he stepped towards her, she turned and gazed up at him through her lashes as she sunk her teeth into her lower lip. He stopped in his tracks, like a deer caught in headlights, as she pinned him with the most alluring look she had and slowly released the lip she held captured.

'Yes, please,' she purred.

He was before her in two steps, his hands gripping her hips tightly as he pulled her against his hard body. She gasped as she stumbled forward and stared up at him with surprised eyes. They'd made love often since that first night weeks ago, but he'd never been demanding, never forceful. He'd been strong and confident in his abilities—as well he should be!—and his language could be colourful when he moaned the things he wanted to do to her—which she loved! —but he often treated her just like the Lady he supposed her to be.

'I keep telling you, princess, you should always wear your hair down.' She heard the little growl in his voice on the word *down* and a thrill ran through her at the possibility of him completely losing control. His hands reached up and pulled out the two clips that were holding her hair in place. As her hair tumbled down her back, Cormac's fingers threaded through it, holding her still as he claimed her mouth.

The kiss was hot and demanding, and Victoria held on to him for dear life. Her knees weakened, and she felt the stone of the handrail bite into her legs as she sought its support.

He softened the kiss, and Cormac's hands slipped from her hair, sliding down over her body, caressing her naked skin. She moaned as his hands slipped over her hips to grab at her backside, pulling her closer.

He hitched her up against him, her legs wrapping around his waist as he carefully positioned her to sit on the edge of the railing. He peppered kisses along her jaw, and Victoria turned her head, allowing him better access, encouraging him to find that spot between her neck and shoulder that drove her wild.

'Do you really want me to make love to you out here?' he whispered in her ear as if someone could overhear them. She knew there were no other guests in the rooms on either side of them, but that didn't stop the thrill of excitement running through her body at the idea of the two of them being overheard or unknowingly watched.

Her answer was a breathless *yes,* and she could feel the

grin of his lips against her skin as he found that spot. She shifted against him, feeling his hard length rubbing against where she needed him the most and moaned in pleasure and frustration at the fact there was still too much between them, stopping her from getting exactly what she wanted.

'Where anyone could catch us?' He kissed along her shoulder as his roving hand cupped her breast before gently easing it out of its cup. She hissed as the cool air caressed her nipple, causing the crowning bud to harden and offer itself to his mouth as he kissed his way to it. 'Any of our guests could spot us, hear us; all they'd have to do is look up.'

The filthy, wanton moan that reverberated through the night did not come from her at the idea of someone spying them, watching them as she took Cormac's hard cock over and over.

'Oh, you enjoy that thought, do you?' he asked before his mouth covered her nipple. She gasped as his tongue swirled over it before his teeth gently nipped it and she thrust her chest at him, seeking more of what he offered.

'What thrills you more?' he asked as he pulled away, dropping to his knees as he continued to kiss and nip his way down her body. 'The idea of being taken out in the open or the idea of someone watching you, catching you. Seeing you do all the naughty things a Lady shouldn't?'

That! her mind cried, but she couldn't seem to get her throat to work to confess such a secret to him, as he carefully wound his arm around her waist to hold her in place as his other slipped beneath her silken panties.

She trembled, her legs shaking as his fingers slipped along her already moist lips.

'I'm waiting, Victoria,' he said, his voice firm. She looked down at him and she was sure he felt the effects of her view on his fingertips. His eyes dark with desire as he stared up at her, her legs casually thrown over her shoulders. His finger stroked her gently, and she shifted her hips forward, trying to seek out the friction she so desperately needed.

'What is it you want more; just to be here or to have someone watching you while I do this?' He slipped a finger into her hot, moist sex and she gave a high pitched squeak, cursing the devilish grin that spread wide on his face. He gently pressed his digit and Victoria closed her eyes, matching each little thrust with one of her own.

'I want—' she began only for her confession to be cut off as his finger moved a little faster.

'Yes?'

'It's the *idea*,' she finally managed to get out. 'Of being caught, of being watched.'

'But you don't actually want to be watched?' She shook her head. 'But the idea of someone knowing you're out here, the idea that they could pull back a curtain and see you looking so lewd, so shameless with my head between your legs, your hands in my hair holding on to me until you got yours… that would—'

'Do it!' she hissed as she stared at him, her hips still working in time with his hand, not actually wanting him to stop. He smiled at her, and leaned forward, stopping a moment to inhale her heady scent before his tongue joined his finger.

The keen that rent the air was loud, and Victoria knew that if the music had stopped at that moment, everyone outside on the terrace below them would have heard her. It made her cheeks flame red, but only heightened the pleasure of what Cormac was doing. The idea of Marcus or one of his guards staring through their gun sight on a rooftop somewhere and seeing her so debauched sent another flood of need coursing through her veins.

What would they think of her, one breast hanging out,

her husband between her legs, the Queen's crown atop her head?

'Cormac,' she cried as his tongue slid from her pulsing bud down to join his finger, seeking more of her taste. 'I'm going to...'

He hummed his approval, and the vibrations sent her over the edge. She came hard, her head thrown back, exposing her neck and chest to whoever might spy them, her legs curling over her husband's shoulders as she pulled him closer, never wanting the pleasure to stop...

She bit back a sob when it came to an end, starring down at Cormac as he slowly pulled away from her.

'You liked that, princess?' he asked, a saucy lilt to his voice. She nodded and continued to stare at him silently as she tried to regain her breath. He gently took her legs from his shoulders and stood up, offering his hand to help her from her perch.

'Glad I could help fulfil your fantasy.'

She licked her lips as she saw the bulge in his trousers. Knocking his hand away, she stared up at him as she reached for his belt.

They were only just getting started...

TO BE CONTINUED

KEEPING HIM SAMPLE

THE ROYALS OF AVALONE - INHERITANCE: VICTORIA PART 3

Available NOW

The messages kept coming.

He'd left his phone behind while they'd gone away on their honeymoon, as had Victoria. They'd enjoyed two weeks on the Royal Yacht, only reachable via the on-board satellite phone which he'd used twice a day to check up on James—who'd had the time of his life with *Auntie Alexi*. At the time, he'd had no idea what the girl was doing to entertain his brother but had been grateful. However, not so much on his return home.

He'd come back to find his brother covered in bruises from adventures such as paintballing, learning how to skateboard, and other such insane activities she'd had the two of them doing. However, he had to grudgingly admit the photographs she'd sent to his phone were adorable.

But that was when he'd seen *the messages*. Several a day

had come through to his phone while he'd been gone. More images of him almost naked, one that suggested he definitely was. The worst was an image taken from a security camera of Geri oiling his shoulders and back where he couldn't reach. It looked highly sexual, even if it was the furthest thing from it; in fact, he was sure the images were from his last night at the club. He was never more thankful than refusing the fluffing service she'd had to offer the strippers than he was at that moment.

He did as Marcus said and messaged the guard with simply, *7-7-7*.

'Happy to be home?' Victoria asked as she came into the bedroom of the penthouse they were still renting, kicking off her high heels before standing before him. 'You know, we have the whole place to ourselves tonight. No James until tomorrow afternoon.'

'What are you thinking?'

'I was thinking,' she said with a wicked smirk. 'That we could christen a few more of the rooms here.'

'Really?' Cormac looked towards the doors that led out to their private sitting room. 'Do you think they're jealous?'

'That these rooms keep getting all the sex? Most definitely,' she said with a solemn nod. 'How about we take a swim?' Cormac's cock instantly twitched at the idea. Since their wedding night, she'd had a bit of a penchant for outdoor experiences. The pool and the sun lounging deck on the yacht had become her favoured places for their fun while they were away. The possibility of them being seen was a thrill for her, even if the crew knew that when he'd told them they wanted *complete* privacy, they weren't to be *anywhere* above deck, not just on the parts they were enjoying. It was the titillation of the idea of someone watching that drove her wild. The fact their pool here was in the open—even if they were at the top of one of the tallest towers in all the land—was obviously giving her the same ideas.

'Want to go *skinny dipping?*' he asked, his fingers slipping under the thin straps of her summer dress before slowly pushing them over her shoulders and down her arms. She breathed in deeply as the dress fell from her torso, exposing her breasts to the air. He lowered his head to hers and kissed her lips before moving to her neck.

She moaned as he kissed just below her earlobe, her hands grasping his arms to keep herself steady as she turned into his touch. His fingers gently stroked up her side, causing her to shiver, her breath turning ragged as he lightly skimmed the side of her breast.

'Cormac,' she hissed breathlessly as she arched her back slightly, trying to get him to touch her properly. 'Please.'

'Now, now, princess,' he whispered in her ear as his other hand reached up to her hair to undo the clip that held it up. 'We're not at the pool yet, isn't that where you want me to *fuck* you?' She moaned wantonly at his words. 'Isn't that where you want your sweet prince to turn you from a royal lady into a common *whore?*'

'Oh, God!' she whimpered before grabbing his face and bringing it to hers. She kissed him with such ferocity that it took Cormac a second to respond in kind. He pulled her against his body, holding her tightly as he poured every ounce of his desire, his love for her, into the kiss.

He pushed the dress down over her hips, so it slid from her body, before slipping his fingers into the sides of her knickers and pushing them down to join the discarded dress.

Her hands moved to his belt, quickly unbuckling it while he worked on his fly. They weren't going to make it to the pool, but he'd ensure he made it up to her afterwards.

'Cormac,' she said against his lips. 'The window.'

'What?' he asked glancing towards the glass. The curtains were open; did she suddenly want them shut?

'I want you to take me up against it.'

'Oh, you are—'

The shrill ringing of his phone made the two of them jump. He frowned down at where he'd thrown it on the bed when she'd come in, and seeing *private number,* he ignored it, pulling Victoria to him to capture her lips again. But when the phone rang out, it started all over again.

The two of them groaned.

'Just answer it,' she said as she turned around. He grabbed the phone, hating the damn device even more, and swiped up so hard he thought he could crack the glass on it, before all but shouting into it, *What?*

He watched Victoria sashay her way towards the window dressed only in her stiletto sandals. She reached the glass pane and turned around, resting her back against it. Her hand slithered down her torso between her breasts, moving down past her navel and into her small thatch of hair that crowned her glory.

'What?' he snapped again, having completely missed whatever it was the person calling him had said. He was enraptured by her fingers slowly moving within her folds, her little gasps of pleasure as she stared back at him with lust filled eyes. She bit her lip as she tried to bite back a moan, but the wanton little sound slipped between them and went straight to his straining cock. 'I'm rather busy right now.'

'I said, you're late on your payment.' Cormac froze as he recognised O'Malley's voice. 'Now put your bride down, tuck your cock away, and get your arse downstairs. I'm waiting.' The line went dead.

He slowly dropped the phone from his ear, staring at Victoria as she posed in front of the window, the sun framing her as a silhouette made it all the more sensual and meant to stoke the fire of desire within him, but at that moment, all it filled him with was ice.

'Get away from the window,' he snapped at her, racing forward and grabbing her by the arm to haul her from the glass.

'Cormac!' Victoria gasped as he grabbed the curtains and pulled them across the window, plunging the room into darkness and hiding them from sight. 'What on earth—'

'Someone was watching,' he bit out, turning away from her as he tucked his now very limp length back inside his boxers and refastened his trousers.

'They were what?' she cried, rushing for her robe and throwing it around her. 'How?'

'I dunno,' he answered honestly. 'I'm going to go and find out what's going on. I won't be long.' He didn't look back as he stormed from the room, cursing up a storm.

He searched for Marcus' number as he pressed the button to call the lift.

'*Hello?*' came Marcus' voice over the line.

'We got a *big* problem,' was all he was able to say before the lift arrived and he hung up.

ALSO BY E V DARCY

The Royals of Avalone - Inheritance:Victoria
Buying Him: Victoria Part 1
Taking Him: Victoria Part 2
Keeping Him: Victoria Part 3

The Royals of Avalone - Inheritance: Henrietta
Beating the System: Henrietta Part 1
Cheating the System: Henrietta Part 2

COMING SOON
The Royals of Avalone - Inheritance: Henrietta
Defeating the System: Henrietta Part 3

The Royals of Avalone - Inheritance: Alexandra
Becoming a Queen: Alexandra Part 1
Playing a Queen: Alexandra Part 2
Crowning a Queen: Alexandra Part 3

ABOUT THE AUTHOR

E.V. Darcy is a former high school teacher with a Bachelor of Arts in Imaginative Writing from Liverpool John Moores University.

She lives in the north of England with her husband and rather large–and very *spoilt*–dog, Jabba, who she rescued in 2015.

When Evie isn't writing you can find her binge watching her favourite T.V. shows, playing computer games, crocheting or cross stitching, or walking her much loved dog.

Visit E.V. Darcy's website for more information on her latest releases and other titbits. Join her newsletter for sneak peeks, first to know about forthcoming releases and discounts on pre-orders!

www.evdarcy.com

Other ways to contact E.V. Darcy:

facebook.com/evdarcy
twitter.com/eviedarcy
instagram.com/evdarcy

Printed in Great Britain
by Amazon